The Final Card
Episode 6
Of
The Missing Shield

Copyright

---

1. http://www.llthomsen.com

2. http://www.twitter.com/LLThomsen1

3. http://www.facebook.com/linda.thomsen.12979

4. http://www.instagram.com/llthomsen

Acknowledgements:

To my husband for his patience and everlasting support that helped me realise my goals and dreams. Though not a geek and fantasy lover like myself, your trust and generosity means the world and this work would simply not have been possible without you.

To the brilliant, most inspiring, most important people of all: to the Owl and the Unicorn - my children; my muses - without whom my imagination would undoubtedly still be slumbering in a deep subterranean cavern. Even when dinner is a little late and I spend hours at the computer you still cheer me on – never lose the magic!

And last but not least: to the readers! Thank you for your interest, support and enthusiasm. Thank you for sticking with me and continuing on this journey – as a 100% indie author, you can never imagine how much this means to me. You make the story telling worthwhile!

Head's up From the Author:

Hi there and thank you for hopping onboard once more.

You will know by now that the lack of glossaries and maps is a deliberate choice on my part as I wanted you to enjoy the read without any distractions.

However, although the maps, glossaries, inventories, etc. are not printed here, it doesn't mean that they don't exist. I mean... this is epic fantasy after all!

So, as a self-respecting fantasy author I have of course elected to support the narrative with everything that will help you 'get your geek on' and I would therefore like to direct your attention to my official website www.llthomsen.com where you may explore titbits about the world of Dallancea at your own leisure, as well as look up names, terms, maps, information about the series - and much, much more.

The Story So Far

> Though she and her team has searched and pulled no stops to locate Princess Iambre's missing life-shield, Solancei, Chief of Security, Eso Mehadja, stands without a concrete clue as to where the feisty Duchess might be located. Forced to reveal that she did not act quick enough when her informants reported trouble on the day of the jackal fight, the Chief has now taken full responsibility for Solancei's predicament, and admits her guilt and regrets to Iambre.

> Iambre's and Mehadja's never-resting fears concerning the Knights Commander Zulavi's involvement crop up once more, and the Chief is finally forced to speak plainly about the reality of their circumstances - including their diminishing chances of rescuing Solancei, should this western lord in fact be at fault.

> It leaves Iambre furious and appalled, but the blunt truth cannot be denied that if things should go wrong, she will have little choice but to throw Solancei to the wolves in order to preserve the pristine reputation of her own name.

> Beset by strange emotions, a desperate Iambre tries her hand as future ruler, demanding of Mehadja that she brings her along on the coming evening's outing to an inn named The Golden Ball. Iambre wishes to be present when the Chief questions a man named Natusse, because this Seinar Natusse (a local information vendor) supposedly has a lead on Solancei. However, much as expected, the Chief pulls rank and the Princess' hashed command is rescinded.

> Desperate as ever after Chief Mehadja's frank words and candid refusal to involve her in the search, Iambre remains certain that she needs to be present in person when Natusse is questioned. Haunted by a strange gut feeling that Solancei is running out of time, she ponders the predicament - a rising impatience riding her. Though unintended, soon, from the Princess' musings a sudden simple but courageous plan starts to form.

> Yet Iambre is not naïve. As Heiress to the Ostravahn throne and as a guest in the conservative Province of Zanzier, she knows she cannot hope to succeed alone and that the bold idea needs the aid of an ally. Amidst all the required secrecy that surrounds Solancei's disappearance, the only person that she can trust, is Bilan Metavo – the Captain of her retinue and would-be lover - and taking a stance and a chance, she summons him. Confiding in him, she holds back only a few sensitive details and for a wonder it would seem that he is amenable to help.

> Simultaneously, elsewhere the Guardian Commander, Malandar, has finally made progress, travelling from Kretoria into Zanzier - courtesy of a ferry crossing that contrary to former experiences did not cause any of the normal side effects that a Spell-Weaver might experience upon contact or proximity with free-running water. Whether this is due to changes in the magic or within himself remains uncertain though, and he is battling unusual feelings that - courtesy of the Maker - should not influence him. Alarmingly, he is not recovering his strength like he once would have done before the magic was torn, nor does he seem able to shake-off the idea that using the Neidar Ba'raie – foul as the plan might be – will probably remain his strongest, and only, chance of success.

> Torn by the state of his surroundings and the abysmal choices afforded him, Malandar cannot seem to mentally reach his fellow Guardians either and fails to make the arranged connection with fellow Guardian Thessilia Emara to receive progress reports. He is ir-

refutably persuaded that there is something wrong with Alérathnar the Maker – otherwise his old-enemy-turned-Guardian, Rhindarhlar Mehand'Arun of the Heirah-Noor Elvern, would not have dared such an open show of lingering animosity back at the Oratorio, nor would the Speaker have been so adamant upon his own quest to visit the Sabén-Heshep Elvern to search their library and the Tapestry for additional information. An encouraging development occurs however, when instead of Guardian Emara, the Ermaron Guardian, Isavelia Cahmerhin unexpectedly reaches out with news that she has located a shard from the sundered Astrolabe.

> Unsure of his own strength to hold the Upper Circle together should the Maker be 'indisposed', and likewise unsure of their fellow Guardians' current persuasions, Malandar agrees with Cahmerhin to keep the discovery of the shard between the two of them. Moments later, and just as unexpectedly, Guardian Emara successfully instigates and opens the link between their minds that Malandar could not, and her concern - though masked - is just a little too insightful.

> Meanwhile, Knights Commander Simarovien Zulavi is busy. His meeting with Lord and ally Visentor Tan'Xaviar has turned up some interesting possibilities in regards to the future use of an old artefact that can be activated by magic to form a circle from which, and through which, communication and even face-to-face meetings can be conducted. However, he still does not trust Visentor – a thing that becomes apparent once more when the Tuxaman Lord unexpectedly decides to throw Zulavi a seemingly random comment about a 'surprise'.

> Advising that Zulavi should monitor his aviary for the arrival of the Red Wing with a golden claw and stand ready, Tan'Xaviar severs the circle's magical field before Zulavi is able to clarify the meaning of the other man's cryptic words. Frustrated and uneasy, Zulavi has no choice but to carry on with his day and the many preparations stacked for his clandestine plans for the future. However, on a

whim, he decides to check up on the still-unidentified female prisoner in the dungeon. She remains tight-lipped, but he intends to change that. If he cannot rattle her, he can force her tongue with the poison known as Megaa'ron – a drug that is both addictive and deadly, not to mention instantly detrimental to the ability of those who can link with the State of Veranto.

> Entering the crumbling depths of the dungeon beneath Castle Zanzier, Zulavi finds that two of his gaolers have made an astonishing discovery. They have stolen a medallion of intricate design from his prisoner, and though angered by their antics, he is instantly mollified when the men offer up the piece for him to keep. He is certain that it can only be fashioned from the coveted metal known as Dragon Silver, but how can this woman be in possession of such a valuable piece? And what does it mean? Zulavi adds his questions to those already in existence, and commands his men to ready the prisoner for the rack.

> Solancei is fluctuating in and out of a strange state of mind. The Veranto cuddles her injuries but her head seems to be uncommonly affected by the extended connection. As a thoroughly ill-advised conduct, she knows her clinging to the Link amounts to abuse, yet she cannot allow herself to relinquish it - both for fear that she will lose it for good and for the pain of her injuries, which would instantly hand Zulavi the means to make her talk.

> The sly theft of her medallion has left Solancei livid, however – it is a loved and cherished gift from Iambre, which means more than money to her - but even this seems to be swallowed by the depth of her affinity as she sinks ever-deeper into herself, thus escaping the cares of the 'outside world' but then also faces the peculiar new pull of a strange, new-found silver light in her core. Not knowing if it's part of her unexpectedly reaching a higher state of her mastery, or whether it's an illusion brought on by her abuse of the Link, she

searches inwards, barely noticing the events in the real world as she is let to an interrogation chamber where the illegal rack awaits.

> Only too late does Solancei realise that Zulavi intends to use the Megaa'ron and that the effects of this will be her undoing as - one way or another - she will then assuredly betray Iambre as well as the Enclave. To sow further grief, amidst her already seemingly-fatal predicament, Zulavi now reveals designs to marry Iambre and make her his queen. It opens a vast cave of fears within Solancei, yet it seems she is sealed to her own fate – something, which does not include shielding Iambre from this hidden threat.

> Iambre is unaware of the danger closing in, and without Solancei to protect her, Zulavi's plans seem destined to succeed...

Zulavi's Designs

LORD SIMAROVIEN ZULAVI, most-trusted and esteemed Knights Comman-der of the Western quadrant, coveted the Princess as his Queen? He... he desired to ruin her friend's life?!

For a moment, Solancei, proven Veranto Master of the 2nd Grade and royal life-shield of Iambre del'Dulac Isthalani Actarione, couldn't breathe for sheer terror. She was freefalling as though pushed from the highest peak of Oriana's Mount – her limbs windmilling as she fell; the air too thin: her heart nearly ex-ploding from her chest as she couldn't seem to breathe...

Then something within her unravelled.

"You insolent bastard!" She spat forth the words as though they were a curse, unable to hold back the pristine, red-flecked anger that ignited from a flash of embers to a galloping wild-fire, "You cannot do this! You cannot-"

Seething with inner venom, her throat seemed to catch on the words but a razor-edged wrath was firing in her core, cutting her without mercy, and she was suddenly heedless of the repercussions.

"The Crown Princess Iambre is not yours to marry you rabid dog!" Keeping her voice low to control the pitch, she reiterated with a basting of ice-coated fury, "What you seek is impossible; illegal! How dare you contemplate Her La-dyship in such a familiar manner!? How dare you speak such fantasies?! Gods, if you have a death wish, then undo these shackles and I'll oblige you!"

So to underscore the tirade, again Solancei yanked the chains that held her prisoner to the rack. *No give! No. Bloody. Give. And she was losing control. She was better than this but couldn't help herself...*

"Gods rot you!" she cussed, voice once more blistering, rising, "If you presume to move on this lewd desire, you will be flocked till the flesh strips off
your backside before they burn you! You... you... you pretentious fool! You...
foul traitor!"

Flustered that she could not find a better insult to match the hate that
seemed to bubble within her at the thought of him ever touching her cousin
and childhood friend, Solancei punctuated the ineffectual spiel with another
brutal yank on her restraints. *No! Give!*

For a blink her world seemed to spin one-eighty upside down: everything
she'd ever been; everything she'd ever known: stripping from her person to become tiny flakes of paper-fine snow - torn and set aflutter in all directions of the
compass by the winds of a sudden, relentless squall – yet one thought remained.
*Klaas! Klaas must learn about Zulavi's plans; the bastard wasn't jesting and she
could not let this happen to Iambre!*

Chilled by the images in her head, Solancei panted angrily, belatedly
pulling the tattered edges of her 'own-self' back in, to form the shell that she'd
need to remain strong. The starlight in her core flashed – hardening her; freezing her resolve into something deadly.

Without slackening the scathing contempt she held for her mad captor, she
fixed her gaze on the man.

"You will burn!" she grated at him again for good measure and unwilling to
relent, "Burn!"

Staring back at her, the pale-eyed man didn't seem to blink for a long moment. In fact, Lord Simaro Zulavi looked semi-frozen by the ferocity of her
near-manic onslaught, but as she bit her lip trying to rekindle a semblance of
calm to see her through this, a slow flush started riding up his neck and angular
cheekbones.

It indicated that her outright insult had clearly touched a nerve after all. It
pleased her to have penetrated his 'metal' where other words had failed and she
used the respite to pull at her restraints again. She felt split in two: one part
contemplating the other half as if she could not comprehend any need for anxiety: as if it was beneath or maybe above her, whilst the other... *the trapped animal...* was growling in fury. *If she damaged herself in the process, she'd not care.
Iambre had no idea... Gods rot the man!*

In her mind, his sure words ricochet like steel off armour – every bounce and hit ringing like a bell of discord in her ears. *My Queen... There will be other gifts... My Queen...*

The words consolidated the two halves of her. 'How could this be happening?' one part of her wailed as it became *her* once more, whilst the other half pushed to absorb, relenting and bending as her emotions merged.

It left her strangely brittle and Solancei knew the beginnings of a deep ache starting to stir at the thought of Iambre alone against this man, but with the Veranto still wrapped around her, at least she felt no physical pain and it gave her heart. *If she scraped her bones raw to get free of these flecking fetters, then that was a price she was willing to pay. Her body would mend. Injuries would heal. If she could just-*

For a moment, her pulse was racing wildly again - as though she'd been running hard. As she re-tested the chain, the manacles rubbed her skin raw; she was probably about to dislocate her bones too, but it was useless – no matter the angle, she could not slip from the irons!

With a hard sound, she expelled the breath she'd held-in whilst pulling.

If she could have, she would have chopped her damn hands off, but those flecking cuffs must have been made especially for a woman because they weren't budging. *But they had to...*

Sawing at her lip with her teeth, she pulled with all her strength just one final time, but even as she fought her own losing battle, panting heavily now, she was acutely aware of Zulavi as he strained to stomp out the anger raised by her crude outburst. In a few blind moments she'd be spent, and yet with every heartbeat, she was expecting him to come at her with some form of brutal reprisal, either in retaliation over her words or else to stop her fudged escape attempt.

He didn't.

Even as she finally admitted defeat with the irons to lie back gasping, he still did nothing more than summon a quick dirty smile of overbearing satisfaction as he glared at her.

He remained angered though. The colour was fading from his cheeks but his eyes were as flat and lifeless as pebbles. Or death.

Closing her eyes for a long blink, Solancei licked her lips tasting blood. Her breathing was returning to normal, and with it, a semblance of her usual, level-headed ability to reason. *Her loss of control had been beneath her; her outburst had been stupid! It would not do to make him wonder, and she feared she'd done just that.*

To navigate around the speculation before he could find the mind to question her extreme emotional response, she spun her former rage into a flimsy feint of mockery and put-on incredulity. "What? Is M'lord surprised now? Well, he most assuredly shouldn't be!"

She swallowed hard. "I am a loyalist! As are you – I know you have to be - and yet you speak like a rebel? Like a traitor?! Because with those words you mark yourself! Gods help us, why else speak of the Crown Princess so? Why else speak as though she is meant to be your wife?! By decree, she belongs to someone else! As a noble, you should know exactly how and why that is! By Belanzia'Cha: our Princess is the Future of the Realm and all that: the peace and the welfare of the joint provinces; you cannot play with that; the succession to the throne already lays clear. You know this, beyond... beyond... everything!"

Solancei trailed off. She was babbling. She knew that – but part of her was seeking to comprehend: to assure herself that it was all just a misunderstanding: that she'd gotten the wrong idea, or-

After her mad outburst, the cell seemed quiet. She collected her thoughts, but seeing his expression, she faltered, already knowing her own folly. She did not want to babble again, yet she could do little to prevent the arrival of true consternation from colouring her voice as she pushed, searching for a reason; for answers.

"I mean, do you presume that the King would look favourably on you?" A rolling stab of false mirth escaped her lips, but she started up again, "Good Gods, is that it? Do you think that His Majesty would alter procedures so as to please you?"

The remnants of her vitreous laughter momentarily disguised her arrival at the crumbling edge of madness, but she could hear the fatal quiver in her voice as she refused to relent, "Why, I simply don't understand your confidence, M'lord. The Princess must be less than a month away from reaching Tuxama. Surely-

"Why surely the mere *suggestion* that *her* hand in marriage should be passed onto *you,* would be taken as some kind of insincere jest?"

Solancei nearly laughed out loud again so as not to choke on her words as she pictured King Kaimar's face but managed to hold on to a measure of control this time. *Kaimar was as calm of spirit as the waters on Lake Etruia - but Gods help them all: he'd reach for the broadsword above that great fireplace in his apartments and slay Zulavi if he as much as heard whispers of such a ridiculous proposal! Unlike some fathers, Kaimar loved his only daughter...*

And yet Simarovien only smiled. Actually smiled: a predator; a Demonai...

Tendrils of cold premonition shot through her gut at the sight. Once again her breath seemed to still in her lungs. *Staring a God in the eye couldn't have left her more fearful...*

"My, my, well who would have thought that you should turn out to be such a believer in Crown and Constitution?" he remarked, the comment ending in something that sounded like salty criticism as he pursed his lips, adding, "So typical of a modern noble... typical... you are all so... so predictable, grey-eyes. Did you realise this?"

His offence obviously evaporating, Simaro tutted and waved his hand at her. "Oh well, it is hardly of any matter what you sound like now. Whether you are a noble or not, I fear not telling you of my views! The Senate? The King? Phew, the whole setup is tiresome! You believe I'm going to ask for Lady Iambre's hand? Oh but how quaint!"

Whilst the starlight in Solancei's core emitted a fractured opaque flare, near-enough burning in its coldness, Simarovien shook his head at her perceived folly, "My dear, you must understand that one does not really ride up to the King of our good realm and *ask* for the Crown Princess! No, that would never do! Indeed, if you want something valuable like that, you rarely have other choice but to take it. That's how the world works, grey-eyes!"

"Like you took me, you mean?" she mouthed as her already cold heart grew colder still. For a new moment her mind went blank once more, the impact of his words leeching all strength from her core - *but for the persistent but unfamiliar starlight, of course.* It couldn't distract though. *Not only was the man ruthless, but it would seem that he was indeed a traitor! It shocked that she was barely shocked.*

"Ah but you and the Crown Princess are two entirely separate matters, let me assure you!" Simarovien waved the words away with one hand as though they were insignificant. "I took you, grey-eyes, because I could, and because of your slight, and because of what I suspected in relation to your knowledge about the State of Veranto. But as for Her Ladyship? Oh well, you needn't concern yourself with the trivialities: it is already set in motion and when we are all done, all that counts is that I will have Iambre Actarione as my wife and Queen! And you know... because she'll feel beholden to me, she'll come around to the thought of being my consort soon enough."

To use the words 'consort' and 'Iambre' in the same sentence did not seem right but although there was something about the way he'd said it that made her imaginary hackles rise, Solancei just couldn't see past the word 'wife'. Somehow the Knight Commander's candid statement landed like a strike where his physical touch had proved ineffective!

And he looked so confident! Solancei's feelings of dread intensified. *It's all been set in motion. Mercy, Iambre...! He must be wrong in the head to utter such a mad statement with so little care! Surely, he must be...*

And yet there was no 'surely' attached to that assertive stance of his, nor to the words that left his mouth. *She will be beholden...*

A sickening wave of aversion rolled through Solancei. Somehow the man spoke with such certainty, with such confidence, that she knew he must be plotting against Iambre for certain, and - *through his plans to marry her* - even against the Throne itself.

And in such an event, what would Kaimar do? What could he do?

Well, the King might seem vague at times: buried to his neck in the affairs of state more often than not, but he was also fiercely protective and he would definitely not tolerate betrayal. If someone harboured thoughts of 'kidnapping' his only daughter and Heiress, it would be perceived as a direct and malicious intent of war, and to tamper with the line of succession too...? *Gods but the guilty parties would hang and burn. Or worse...*

The ice in her core crystallized. *If Zulavi committed such an act, there were all the chances that Kaimar would not hesitate to bring down the entire royal army on Zanzier. And what then? What could Zulavi hope to achieve? What was he not saying?*

Solancei swallowed hard. It seemed like an impossible thing to contemplate. Zulavi and Iambre... *Gods, but how could he truly fancy himself as Iambre's consort? Was he in love with her? Was that it?*

Solancei knew that many a man might be accused of harbouring such feelings for the Heiress – some pure, some less so - but for some reason, that very thought in relation to Zulavi had her cringing in revolt. *She could not imagine Zulavi loving anyone like that. He seemed colder than a Wilkaran Snake and... and as for Iambre?*

Feeling obscene, Solancei nearly smiled. *Well, Iambre would most definitely not want this man! Not beholden or otherwise!* As matters stood, Iambre barely even wanted the mantle of her birth, nor her treasures, nor her comforts. *Iambre Actarione only wants Bilandro Metavo,* she thought. *Zulavi does not know, but she'll tell him. He does not know this either, but he will soon learn that Iambre is far more than merely 'eccentric'. He'll discover that the stubborn woman would rather die than go willingly with a traitor!*

Solancei quivered, fear rolling her stomach; making her nauseous. *No matter what the bastard might say or think, Iambre would be sure to put up resistance: she would not the easy prize he believed her to be and when he realised this, Iambre would get hurt!*

Inhaling sharply, she swallowed the million pinpricks of sharp anxiety that seemed to race along her body regardless of her tenacious hold on the State of Veranto.

The thought of the medallion's fate returned. *What if Zulavi were to dangle the necklace in Iambre's face with the hope that its worth and rarity might sweeten her? Then she'd-*

Solancei stopped herself just shy of yanking the chains again. *There'd be no question of the outcome! Iambre would recognize the necklace for sure! In fact, between the threat of the Meer'ron and Iambre's reaction, it was perhaps now a simple race against time in which would give Solancei away first!*

Now, in turn, what might just come of that, did not bear thinking about! It would be a flecking disaster! Zulavi didn't know this - *couldn't know, of course* - but trouble would spread like wildfire across autumn dry fields! Solancei's secret would be out, her identity revealed, along with the circumstances under which Simaro had caught her - and the scandal, and the 'currency' of this valuable information...

To keep the Princess blame-free, Zulavi would exact a price. A price, which might just be enough to-

But that cannot have been his plan, she recalled, *he didn't know you, nor of your connections with Iambre, and yet... and yet it hardly mattered now. What came next would invariably fit right into his scheme all the same, and-*

Solancei's core flared with a burst of coldness so pure it made her breath catch as a streak of panic sawed through her. *Oh Gods, she had to get out of here! Iambre would not have a clue that she was in danger! Of course, she wouldn't! Solancei was supposed to be her Shield and now...*

Unspoken but ever-present in Solancei's mind - like some small leech deeply embedded within – was the thought of failure; the thought of the possibility that one day she might not be good enough, or fast enough, or strong enough, to matter! It had been riding her, of course, ever since she'd sworn the words of servitude and signed her name, and if never a great fear nor a debilitating one, it was nevertheless a fear which had continued to stalk her duty as Iambre's Shield. For how could it not? *To fail a friend... her only friend... to not even be there...!*

For a moment her anxiety almost unravelled everything. *The idea of Zulavi-*

She battled the feelings, hauling on the Link angrily. *She had to believe that if he wanted Iambre for a wife, then at least he would not wish to harm her, true? Except, that there were many different ways of harming someone. Many. Some Zanzierian women were put into solitude... some-*

She pushed the image brutally aside. She could not afford to go there!

"So in your efforts to see Princess Iambre wearing your marriage torque, you would bring down war on the Provinces?" she enquired tonelessly though she watched him carefully - stamping mentally on her fluctuating feelings as though they were a bunch of cockroaches.

It worked to a point, except that just like the roaches, the more you killed, the more you attracted.

Overruling the spikes of fear, she continued, "Her Ladyship is rumoured to be well-loved, you know; the realm would be in uproar. Is one princess really worth that much to you?"

"Oh invaluable," he replied lightly, "Though not for the reasons you'd think. Indeed the fact that she is popular is but a helpful coincidence that will see me solidify the link between old and new. The people will like that because the people like *her* and what she represents. And as for war...? Well, wars come and go – don't they? Some bloody, some of paper and pen and words, some more subtle. You might be uneducated in these matters, but one could argue that we are already at war: at war with the Senate; at war with these modern traditions that we try to hold dear, yet secretly know to be worth nothing as it is but a set of shambles upheld to gloss over what goes on behind those damned Etruian gossamer curtains! The bribes, the corruption, the underhanded distribution of power, the impotent Crown, the 'stale' Senate?

"Progress has turned stagnant and War is in the very air we breathe. War - and the absolute need to remember the ideals we once revered! Come it as it may, *I will* restore us to The Golden Age! Come as it may, Iambre Actarione *will* wear my marriage torque! I have support and I intend to use it. My claim will be realised and the rest is but a formality."

Astounded, Solancei blinked. His words deflected her personal fears like nothing else - which was just what she'd needed. *Zulavi was demented!* How could he say such things about the realm? How? The Gods must have clouded his eyes and addled his mind, otherwise, how could he simply stand there and speak such things without guilt or conscience? His plans seemed twisted, mind-buckling, skewed... *And they were bound to fail!*

Had he forgotten how the Chaos Wars had nearly destroyed them all; had he forgotten how since the Treaty of Unity, the realm had prospered and grown, and – on the whole, known peace? How could he think that corrupt or stagnant? Had he even been to the Etruian capital recently? Had he read about the laws passed and the money distributed?

It left her baffled. Progress was everywhere. And not just to benefit the capital but for the good of the entire realm. New aqueducts were being built to lead the overflow of spring waters from the Teeth of Land's End to the three reservoirs being excavated to serve the year-round dry Plains of Pendrosa. There was the diversion of Senate funds to serve the Nomads of The Yellow Snake to help them develop new, secret routes to link theirs with Zanzier and Deb'Aran in order that their trade of the coveted Afhpar horse could develop. All of this was possible only because the realm had been moulded into an elected democracy, whereas this 'Golden Age' he'd mentioned...?

Well... she had never even heard of it - and she'd read a lot of books, nosed through countless scrolls and visited numerous museums where relics from before the Chaos Wars figured heavily on display in warning and remembrance - and sometimes both!

"So you'd kidnap the Princess, usurp the King and start a new regime," she summed up, needing to say something; anything. "How? When? It all seems rather... ambitious. And who would rule then? Who'd be King? One of the Senators? Another Lord? You?"

Crossing his arms to assume a laid-back stance, Zulavi's lips arched: a lazy hairpin curve of sustained surety. Rather than answering, he said, "I think me all this talk has diverted us both for long enough in one day. When the Meer'ron makes you more pliable we shall speak again in more detail, but not before. As I have told you already: I don't have long. Not today. Not in the foreseeable future. This day alone will fly. Soon I will be escorting the lovely Crown Princess to the nightly banquet - yet before I go get busy with the daily tasks, I should like nothing more than to witness you enjoy that precious first dose of Meer'ron. You'll find there's... well, that there is nothing quite like it, I'm told - and I would be there to see you 'ride the red' before I leave you in my men's capable hands. Call it whimsical, but I feel entitled."

Watching him through slit eyes, Solancei somehow couldn't quite concentrate on his words. Somehow the Enclave and the State of Veranto were just not as important as thinking about Iambre and how she might best serve her friend in her present predicament. Even the thought of the Meer'ron and what it would do could not make a difference. Could she offer him something else to make him reconsider his original bargain with her? Something he'd accept of equal worth?

Perhaps, yes; perhaps maybe. She would not trust him to honour it though, however, it would buy time. Still, whatever she chose to offer up it would need to be something to make him stand up and take note. *Nothing short of sacred,* she felt. *Something like... like where to find the Enclave?*

Now such an answer would buy herself time perhaps, but not Iambre. And anyway... could she truly consider betraying her connection to the Enclave in exchange for a dubious amount of time and a shady outcome? It would serve little - least of all in a sense that might make the sacrifice worth it to herself or Iambre!

So could she pretend it wouldn't matter? And would he even care, regardless? The Meer'ron would give him all he wanted anyway - and if the stories held truth, she wouldn't be able to stop herself.

She shivered.

Without more information, it seemed nigh on impossible to determine the most valuable path forward. His mad plans for Iambre could be set to spring into motion tonight or a month from now - there was no way of knowing, and if she kept asking, he'd develop suspicions where there were currently none. He'd said he had support. *Whom?* Perhaps it was some unaffiliated noble who stood ready to aide him? *Or several?* Or perhaps even another Knights Commander - though from the way he spoke of Commander Tahais Isoho, she doubted the two men shared enough love to cement that type of alliance!

Solancei glanced at Zulavi's face again but it seemed to her that a film had crossed her eyes, softening her vision, causing his face to blur in the light. Feeling wretched, she blinked - and was surprised to feel the touch of warm liquid spill from the corners of her eyes, down her temples. Pain cut into her heart: the kind of pain that the State of Veranto was not known to protect against; in her core the bright starlight seemed to blaze in line with her hurt and she somehow understood she could reach for it and put an end to it all - but at what cost to Iambre and the Realm? *Mercy... she needed to think! Needed to think...*

She didn't see how she could possibly stop him for long enough to help Iambre escape his plans. Maybe Zulavi would keep her here indefinitely and she would never be able to do more than weep. Or maybe he would kill her, and she'd die knowing what she'd done; and what she hadn't!

It gave free reigns to emotions she'd believed under tight lock; more tears stalked... *the fiercest predators on a dark night...* nothing as simple as self-pity, nothing as plain as fear for herself, no - it was all for the *understanding.* Vengeful Gods, she had never feared her own future: not the next hour, nor tomorrow or the day after that - but for all of her training, Klaas had never provided her with a scenario like this and she had no idea... *no idea what she should do!*

She blinked, blinked again, and forced the numbness of Veranto to bottle away the tears that showed on the outside; Zulavi looked expectant now; as if he'd just broken her... and in a way perhaps he had because there was little comfort to be taken from the knowledge that this would not end well; that all she might have left was the measure of the defiance that had always curled itself around her core, causing her trouble. *And Gods... his face seemed the only thing she'd looked at for an eternity.* She had no idea what to do, no – but if all she had was defiance and will, then perhaps...

It was risky; it was an act of betrayal in itself just to be contemplating the idea but if she could make it work... if the State of Veranto did not fail her... if...

Well, if she could do nothing more for Iambre, then this would have to do! *Iambre, I'm sorry...*

"No!" she said aloud to no one in particular, her voice void of the New Wood accent she'd tenaciously clung onto till now.

It felt peculiar to embrace the finality of her decision; of her situation. Her tone reflected deadened emotion and voided the aching sadness that now began to vibrate within her core in alignment with every breath she pulled. *Regrets were for those who would live, though. Duty came first! Always! And if she could find that level of Veranto she'd enjoyed earlier, then perhaps... then perhaps she might try this one final thing... she might...*

At the thought, a deep fear ate at her innards as though they'd been dipped in the acidulous venom of a red viper but it wasn't a fear that could compete with what she felt if she did not make the attempt because her friend's life was on the edge! Chief Eso – Klaas - had to be warned and she must try this. *No, not try! Do! And so, by the Back of the Beyond: let Inkar'Chi spit her in the eye - see if she cared, for she must do this! Must!*

She'd never done anything like this before, though; had never pushed her skills that far before, and she knew that she might have to stumble her way through with disastrous effects, and still...

And still she had to try her utmost to succeed because there was no more time. The Meer'ron was coming...

Solancei shut her mind away.

"No." she repeated in the same tone as before - as if to get the persuasion straight in her own mind - then drew a deep breath that would have been impossible, she knew, without the State of Veranto to cancel out her injured ribcage. *If only I can remember...*

"No, you will ruin everything," she told him, "And so I fear that I cannot tell you what you wish. I cannot and I will not and your plans will be ashes."

Solancei let herself float to become as light as a speck of dust drifting in the golden midday sunbeams emitted through the wooden slats of her Etruian palace apartments. Unlike the dust, she had a purpose though; a destination - and as she relaxed, she allowed her consciousness to sink deeper into herself till there seemed little left of her but her own name and her connection to the Link.

It was a comfortable state of mind, however, and to do this she needed the distance: needed the objective insight that would allow her to think back to an event long past. *Now what exactly had that scroll said? She recalled the formal prose; the nine – or was that ten? – 'Signifiers'... but now as for the exact context...?*

Somewhere outside her limit of care, Simarovien exhaled sharply through his nose, a hiss of air that translated his disbelief as surely as any words of anger. Next to the fire-pit, she heard the sentiment echoed by the one remaining cajoler in the shape of an unintelligible, half-formed gasp of words, but already she was pulling away from reality through the Link with *Veranto.*

'Out of all the scenarios: not the final, you envisaged', a snarky, laconic part of her commented, but she paid it no heed. For one crystal clear moment, she saw Simarovien's glacier eyes narrow with concern, but then she dismissed him too, zoning in now instead on the uniform groves of the ceiling where the evidence of workmanship appeared oddly out of scale. *You know what Zulavi is about to do. What he will be forced to do now! Perhaps you've even known all along. But it cannot matter! He still thinks his, the winning hand of course, because in a way it is, and that is fine too - if only you can go deep enough. Now the scroll had been clear on the process she must follow... if only she could recall...*

Feeling afloat, she sensed Simarovien's emerging ire but she didn't care. It was like a gnat throwing itself against a wall. *This man was nothing - Iambre was everything!* Her core was a sparkling brightness but she'd not wanted to look that way: it hadn't felt true, and now, thankfully, she needn't go that far...

Solancei smiled. *So, he thinks he knows about the State of Veranto, does he? Well, the bastard hasn't seen a fraction yet! Not a fraction!* Her final card was about to hit the table... double ace if this worked; jesters if not... but in a way he'd never perceive possible, she had to fight just one final time and all she 'needed' was to rekindle the appropriate memories; all she had to remember were a few particular paragraphs. Of course, she'd long tried to forget everything for fear that Klaas would indeed realise that she'd broken, not only student/mentor confidence by snooping, but also the Veranto Enclave's trust by disregarding a Master's word, so-

Solancei's smile widened a fraction as her sense of irony deepened. *The things she'd learnt from that scroll had not been hers to know yet – and officially she should not have acted on her desires to know such a secret, but perhaps this would be her redemption? If she could protect Iambre...*

Sure, for this to work, she'd need more luck than Fabrano Icolor himself on the final day of combat when he and his men had faced the Insurgent Hordes outnumbered five to one! But - *as everyone knew* - Icolor had famously gone on to win the battle: he'd slain Phudor and ended the Chaos Wars – all in one day! *Not bad!*

Of course what such a feat must have cost him with the Spinner of Luck Herself, one could only dread to speculate, and in comparison, this was nothing! Now surely a little help might not be too inconceivable? *After all, Lady Goddess,* she half-thought, half-prayed, *have I not entertained you fabulously already?*

Well, in her own view she had, but Kira'Cha remained as silent as ever. It was hardly a surprise but if Solancei could still not count on a little divine intervention, she could at least rely on her own resolve. *And I must do this! With or without the help of Gods or man, I must warn Klaas!*

She yielded a little further, feeling strangely heavy in her own skin, but then even this evaporated and she was... free...

Darkness cloaking her, only one conscious word seemed to stick. *Scroll! Scroll...*

The word became a sentence; a feeling; a design; focussed, she slid towards it. *Now all she had to do was remember the specifics of that scroll – that was all – yet fortunately for her, the State of Veranto was just about the correct medium for invoking a near perfect recall, and Zulavi...*

No, Zulavi hadn't seen anything yet, but he would. She hoped...

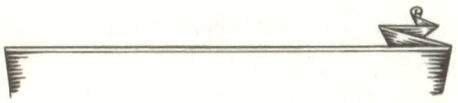

Silicia'Cha's Deluded Fools

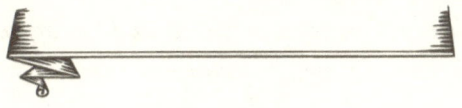

I WONDERED IF THERE were problems again...

The copper-haired Guardian Thessilia Emara's hesitant question echoed into the First Guardian's mind, her sense of humour so obviously not involved, though Malandar Cor'Esardan Denarlin might have embraced inspiration to accuse her of the opposite. In fact, his fellow Guardian's mindful intent was like a ripple of disturbance in the air: suddenly so obvious to Malandar that even if he hadn't felt her sincerity, the lilting care with which she applied tact, actually warned him that she worried to offend or indeed go too far.

It was a realisation that almost startled him because such sensibilities had rarely tamed her in the past, but if it was a display of unusual conduct now, he also perceived just how uneasy her spirit - and mind - 'felt' to interfere with his. It was enough of a revelation, that even had he minded the intrusion, he would've forgiven her.

Wasting little more time, the First Guardian relaxed his mind fully towards her.

"No... No, there are no problems. You are within your right to seek me out. This is the time we agreed, past it even, but I was...' Malandar paused to rush-search his mind for some acceptable excuse that would not heighten Thessilia's strain but found none.

'I was contemplating strategy,' he told her instead and felt her curiosity spike though she said nothing. To put her off the scent for the moment and to placate her, he continued, *'By all means, I think we can dispense with a little formality anyway. The present state of the Ostravahn flows does not allow me the freedom to do anything with ease. Evidently, the initial contact comes easier if instigated from*

your end. If you can reach me without problem, then perhaps this is the procedure we should observe until matters alter.'

'*Very well, Commander,*' Guardian Emara answered, now without any infliction of emotion, '*but if we do this, you should know that the Speaker will not be pleased. Too much is already lapsing, he feels. By the same token, however, he too acknowledges the difficulties we've encountered and has agreed that you may need to communicate with him via myself – and vice versa. Just for now, you understand! So, with this in mind, he has also asked me to inform you - in the event of 'complications' - that he's met someone that he thinks will-*'

'*Wait-*'

Malandar clipped her trail of information short, unconcerned with reproach as a sudden puzzling tingle down his back diverted awareness. It was but the slightest touch of 'wrong' but it was enough to cause disquiet and without guilt he let Thessilia slide further from attention as she became instantly secondary to him.

It proved a wise decision, when less than a blink later, the Spirit Rune at the base of his skull flared into life with such force that it sent a jagged spear of fiery warning down his spine. *All undiluted magic, it made his bones tingle and his fingertips blacken as they crackled with the surplus of power that rushed through him, gathered in an instant to await his Persuasion...*

Without mind but for the shape of the Rune Call, instinct swelled: a feeling of danger so intense now that he wholly expected to look up and see an army of Venzoians tearing towards him!

Hit by spiking surprise to be caught so off-guard, every fibre of his world widening... readying...

Malandar whipped his head around, and-

And saw nothing!

Impossibly, it immobilised him - the runes still singing a song of danger along his spine, though his eyes could locate no enemy with which to contend. *Crazy... the warning and the visual obviously conflicted! But which impression was wrong?*

Malandar's senses clouded on a moment of red-drenching concern. There was no magic here that he could detect; no hidden spells or traps to account for the way he was left both dazed and ready – and still he was distracted by the buzzing warning of danger he continued to experience.

Alérathnar's Runes did not lie. This seemed... impossible...

In his fractured state of mind, he almost missed the attack when it came; missed the minuscule sound of someone approaching, the barely-heard shuffle of footsteps clearly masked by design as someone crept forth with undeniable stealth. But renewed danger registered then - spreading like fine veins of shock throughout his body, just a split heartbeat before Thessilia Emara's incoherent yell of warning cut through his head like a scythe as she perceived of the closing threat also, courtesy of their mental connection.

Fuzziness burned from his mind in an instant: fog erased by more than sunlight. Then instinct and reaction connected and he shut Thessilia's presence from his mind just as the sour stench of unwashed Human enveloped his senses, finally giving credence to warning. *By the seven Venzoian casts!*

As if his world had been hit by a weave to dull all physical reaction, everything seemed to slow as the pitted edge of a metal blade came whispering forth like a Shade, threatening contact with his neck!

Still kneeling from his repose, Malandar didn't pause think, however, as he shifted his balance to twist from the attack – the movement becoming a blur to belie his wronged senses, just as he reached back over one shoulder to curl the fingers of his right hand around Heruvar's long smooth hilt-

...iron nicked him... just... the touch of serrated imperfection all-too-real against his skin, but he never stopped moving. Reflexes honed by memory to respond and retaliate, he was poised to draw the sword, but the magic was faster still...

Within a fraction of a blink, he pulled down Focus - his mind connecting without thought to draw from the patterns at his right eye and temple the eligible flows he commanded, courtesy of the Maker, and the magic came in an instant rush of sensation – rising; swelling; greeting...

The Weave an unconscious effort, the Persuasion obeyed: releasing the spell into life, and-

Battle Runes exploded into form then and with an arid blast of Power, he repelled the man who'd cut him: savagely and with enough force to fling the offender backwards as though he'd been hit by the butt of a battering ram at full tilt. It was simple habitual self-defence and without pause to investigate the outcome, Malandar whipped towards the next real threat... *evaluating...*

All at once, Alérathnar's power was rolling in his veins like sweet distraction; like a toxin - begging to be spent now, but his hand on the hilt of Heruvar semi-anchored him, as did the black stain of live magic on his fingertips.

Another blink was all he needed.

He remembered caution then, which aided him to recall that he must spare energy when possible, and with the details of his enemy finally etching themselves into perception, he wrenched a hold of himself. *This would need no magic.* Two scruffy-looking Human men of indeterminable age were running towards his position in a full-on contest to engage him; behind their 'vigorous' approach, yet more men appeared, closing ranks even as he watched them clumsily navigate the 'danger' of the heinar bushes with little sense of caution.

From the state of their clothes, weapons and general un-kept appearances, he immediately categorised them as renegades; yet from the particular stench of incense that wafted in the air towards him - *almost as sentient-aggressive as the men themselves* - he also knew that this was no ordinary gang of robbers. Indeed, the stench a real signature, it struck him they must be one of those packs of lunatics who preyed on lone travellers or caravans in 'honour' of Silicia'Cha, 'Goddess of Love'.

Of course, there was no honour – nor 'love' about it! They named themselves 'The Elated' - in itself a ridiculously twisted choice of term - but the first account of their menace was well over a hundred years old now and the practice apparently still on the rise - at least, if he dared trust his memories from the Long Sleep.

Affronted by their mettle, a sliver of incredulity forked through Malandar; almost, he could not believe peoples' stupidity sometimes. *Almost...*

For an enticing eternity, the magic of his runes beckoned again - *In less than a dozen breaths they'd cut him down* - but he'd have no need of it for this... *it was not worth the waste... no Venzoians here, just a total of nine men... minions of the Mad Ones, yes... Chaos thick in the air all around them; like a wave of grief: they'd done this kind of thing before... but they were blind... and slow...*

The First Guardian received a blood-thinning picture of mental cohesion: their avid conviction of right held the makings of madness within, but it posed no serious threat – at least not to him, for not only did the two men in front attack with more brawn than skill, they had also placed themselves too near each other for the assault to have the desired effect, but still...

The First Guardian felt their auras reach for him as if they carried magic. Their grossly unintelligible battle-cries were marred by accent and excitement that meant nothing to Malandar, and yet the sound somehow got to him: hit him like a physical thing against his already overloaded senses, and...

And that smell... Stupidity defend... It was all he needed...

He stilled for a breath and looked away - for one perfect moment of peace, centring himself whilst the cool affront against his Guardian-ship grew deeper, sharpening... *sharpening...*

It lasted a breath, then the searing icy wrath simply folded back in on itself, purged from existence to leave only a crystalline sense of purpose that rendered all surprise, or anger, or offence, irrelevant. *Silicia'Cha's rank stench filled the air: a stench that now intensified and seemed to burn his nostrils as though he'd been surprised by the Deity in the flesh and not a mere bunch of her zealots.*

It made him briefly wonder how he could've missed it when the runes initially flared in warning, but this too, was of no matter. The first man was on him, the second a mere twinned heartbeat behind, but Malandar was already drawing Heruvar – the move as he rose to his knees bringing up the blade, a single sinuous act that made the sword flash like liquid silver as it met the broad curve of the assailant's axe just as it arched forward to cleave his head.

The collision jarred; it was instant: rising angry sparks off both weapons, but it was the renegade who issued the yelp of pain then, for his strike against Heruvar turned the half-moon head of his seemingly solid weapon into crumbling clinker, the destructive force of kinetic energy riding like a storm back up the shaft and transferring into his limbs with as much forgiveness as an actual hit.

It made the man stagger for a blink: as though he'd been struck by something heavier than a modest sword; it offered space and Malandar didn't waver.

Gaining one foot, he pressed his advantage forward in pursuit, rotating his wrist a fraction to land two succinct injuries before turning Heruvar like a fan to throw back the second renegade and simultaneously press contact on the reverse-spin by slicing into the first man's right humerus... *severing...*

The initial yelp became a thin scream then, as blood sprung: a gory fountain - *red as a sunset in Aellnaron* - and the First Guardian did not pursue the man as he fell from further conflict clutching at the damage. The second assailant, drove forward, already swinging his blade back into the fray, yet cursing nervously - though if it were for the sight of blood or the development as Malandar made the transition from kneeling to upright with a fluid surge of grace and calculating instinct, only he would know.

Oaths flying sparks by the taint of Silicia'Cha's touch, the Guardian whipped his sword around to deflect the slicing lateral attack of the other man's blade, then flowed to engage the attacker directly with a clipped diagonal cut that feinted in below the antagonist's next swing to connect with cloth and flesh in a way that would ensure certain success, and the man fell from his presence with barely a sound.

By now, senses warned the First Guardian that the man he'd initially repelled might soon be gaining a second wind but it was yet not of pressing concern; the third and fourth 'fortune seekers' were looping in with synchronised steps and Malandar settled, unwaveringly awaiting the next clash.

All fractious curses of revenge, they looked only too ready to carve a piece of him - but as their hatred stuck him before all other contact, it only served as an aide to his Guardian instinct, which proceeded to collapse the moment beautifully into a frame where his sharpening vision and narrowing focus finally served to shift the small remainder of his still-ruffled equilibrium back into perfect alignment.

And Time seemed to stretch then... his detachment widening...

Stilled by the calm, Malandar awaited their attack with the patience of a fishing crane poised over the pond in a sacred garden, barely appraising the men now as they split 'formation' to rush him suddenly from both left and right. *One man was slightly faster... it was incidental...*

Seizing Heruvar's lacquered hilt in a double-handed grip, the First Guardian diverted a slicing chop, stepped left and cut right... *horizontally*... and felt the blade glide leisurely through air before impacting... *first flesh, and then something harder, and then air again...*

Still moving, he ignored the ensuing heavy thud as the body fell.

Side-stepping to retreat one pace he avoided the next assailant's sword: extended towards his gut with the undisguised intention of running him through.

The blade missed its target by less than a hand span, but Malandar did not pursue. The fool-man was committed, could not move fast enough to alter his own trajectory, and the First Guardian's attention was already with the next assailant even though swearing and livid frustration seemed to colour the air even stronger than Silicia'Cha as the neglected challenger stumbled past like a breath of wind, intentions rescinded.

It didn't distract; the next gang-member was trying to trace his steps in a circle to attack with the metal-butt of a quarterstaff from Malandar's blind angle. This one with the 'stick' was of smaller stature than his companions, his steps neat and contracted as though he would pounce like a panther when least expected; expertly, he'd raised the staff high on a slanted vertical - as though the plan was to clubber their 'victim' in the face at the first opportune moment.

He might just have managed, Malandar supposed, *but with a Guardian, the stealth was wasted.* He felt the other man's presence like a stain against the continuous warning flare of his Spirit Rune and he moved without error now, embracing his own actions and reactions without thought. Silicia'Cha's stench might be everywhere, yes - but they were not even attacking him fast enough to warrant drawing Silviata as well and rather than waste the breath, he enticed the man to come at him whilst he turned slightly sideways to glance towards the one he'd sidestepped and the one he'd repelled...

Quite as expected, the man with the quarterstaff rushed in... *too slow...*

Malandar exhaled... brought Heruvar up and around...

Moving in a blink-between-blinks, the resilient blade cut the quarterstaff neatly in half and he had already wiped the smirk from the antagonist's sure face a fraction before he twirled Heruvar around to step forward...

Steel penetrating cloth and flesh without obstruction, the antagonist's expression changed yet again then, his mouth forming a near-silent 'o' of surprise now, whilst - for a fluttering heartbeat – the two of them remained locked together face to face, close enough for the First Guardian to feel the man's spicy breath of cheap Imkarahian tobacco on his cheek. Then Malandar pulled back with a wrench and subtle twist to separate.

Afflicted by a slight ripple of contempt, he eyed the now bulgy-eyed assailant without a sliver of remorse for the ensuing blood-cloaked gasp it drew forth as Heruvar slid free to release a plush rush of ruby fluid.

A heartbeat...

The man dropped the ends of his ruined staff to clasp both hands against the new well in his stomach, seemingly still surprised – or perhaps in denial. For a moment watering flat-blue eyes flared to beseech, then the renegade dropped like a side of prime beef off the tail-end of a wagon, muscles quivering, but seemingly unconscious.

Stupid, Malandar thought. *Stupid having to conserve his power in the manner of an ancient winged wurm trying to hoard its treasure for jealous fear it might suddenly disappear! Stupid to be reduced to this: knowing that if he used magic, the cost might cut him later! Stupid.*

Reflexes bunching, he turned from the image of a crouching dragon as well as from the withering man at his feet. The presence of the next threat loomed and yet it was almost over before he'd made a concerted effort to lift his blade into position.

The man who'd overshot his kill when Malandar sidestepped him, rushed in for another try.

Unlike before, he remained silent, though again he attacked with no apparent concern for discipline, and as Malandar repeated his move from round one, the man yet again seemed surprised that his target did not know how to stay still.

It didn't make a difference. On this pass, Malandar gave him no grace; no time to ponder the mistake, as Heruvar swept forth in the wake of his scramble... *twice... like a scythe... severing tendons, muscle and bone...*

The man stumbled just once. Then he folded mid-stride: a felled paper oak landing face-down in a clump of shallow grasses. *Immobile.*

With the smooth elegance and dangerous grace inherited from his mixed ancestry, Malandar angled himself towards the remaining renegades, and for a blink, the world fell quiet.

Then he took a step forward...

Somewhere Between Dreams and Veranto

"WHAT WILL SHE DO? Milord, what will she do? She's all-"

"I said, be quiet you fool! Be quiet and let me observe this!"

From somewhere 'outside' her realm of care, Solancei heard Knights Commander Zulavi speak the order to his crony, but the words seemed unintelligible, as though she was listening to a foreign language that she'd once known but no longer recognized with any of her former fluency. Translation was slow; delayed; her point of reference seemed skewered because she was focussing so intently on her purpose, but it was enough of a distraction that the perfection shifted to ripple and push.

For some hated reason, the quiet words cost her the depth of concentration she'd cultivated. If she hadn't floated so cleanly within herself she might have named her renewed scramble for control 'perversely desperate', but to gather herself thus and to draw deeply enough back into the Link that she might be able to recall the crucial sliver of information she needed before too late, a part of her was suddenly too busy fighting the return of thoughts – and thereby doubts.

If he got the Meer'ron before she could do this, Iambre would be lost. Everything would be lost! And Gods... Klaas had every right to flay her for this, but...

Mentally flailing, she lost a little more of the blissful edge she'd just held. *It was probably moon-shot to even think that she might be able to follow some instructions of an old scroll - even if she was accurately able to recall them there'd be no guarantees...*

Another sliver of dazzling fear moved through her. It was of course similar to what she'd known before: that should she actually succeed in this, it might very well cost her *all* of her ability, because to open herself this wide; to seek out the depth needed, there was a very real chance that she might just burn out her skill beyond repair, and the loss-

The loss would be catastrophic to her; to forever lose the very asset she'd always depended on to lend her the edge over others in strength, stamina, clarity, calm...

Frayed emotions clashed, but ultimately Zulavi would wreak the same results with his poison. It was a saunter along the edge of her own deep-seated fear; it was staring sanity in the eye, then turning her back and relinquishing, but...

But whatever she might do to herself through her garbled unadvised tampering with the State of Veranto, it was nothing in light of what she imagined Zulavi would do to her – and to Iambre, and to the entire realm! Honour and loyalty – *the sanctity of friendship* - demanded of her that she must try and contact Eso; that she must at the very least *try* to use the Veranto to recall. *Gods, and if done right, the exercise would serve to punch through the layers of time that stood between now and then; she'd seen the scroll with her own eyes; read the words...*

Determination and courage were all it took – *she prayed* - but it'd been a long time since she'd read the rules of this procedure. Could it be, maybe too long?

No! No this would not do! The doubts could not be allowed to fester!

Shakily slowing her intake of air, she stilled and reached inwards again. For mercy, the Veranto was perfectly accommodating, however, and as she sank a little deeper still, it was useful not to care how she might find her way back up again. Perfect memory still eluded, but she hadn't expected herself to get in deep that quick a second time – and yet...

In less than a blink, her focus was strengthening: something starting to surface: snippets of conversation that snapped back into mind; general bits of theory discussed during a daily bout of sword-tests suddenly amalgamating into the very clear memory of a plan for a two-person clandestine midnight search of Klaas' quarters...

Inching herself into the memory a little more, the clarity sharpened. *It was disconcerting. And exhilarating.*

Her Link swayed wildly for a moment as she stared in wonder, the infinite perfection of the construct in her mind, now surrounding her like a grand landscape she might walk through if only she could hold the strands together. There were people surrounding her, going on their daily business as though they were unaware of her presence. If was peculiar. Then she realised they were secondary: extras in a play, shadows against her mind though she recognised some of their faces, and the colours of their garbs, and caught snippets of their conversation; a golden-red finch sang thrills from the branch of a nearby Opadin tree: fruits ripe, hanging low, ready to harvest...

Memories came faster then, rewarding her sharp attention, bunching up within her - almost as if there was too much detail to bring to mind and not enough room to contain it – but as she allowed the stream to roll unbound through her head, the panicked feeling wilted to allow her choice over the se-lection.

She 'skipped' forward, allowing the scenery to blur and alter as she manipu-lated the jumps in time. Now, what she wanted to bring forth, was the specifics of the one night where she'd been looking for the scroll from which her men-tor had read aloud some of the complex theory behind one Master's ability to place himself into contact with another: illicit details she'd since then deliber-ately tried to forget, as it were.

Solancei joggled for a moment, on the brink of collapsing the hard-won Link. She felt the intended memory slide as if it refused to stay logged in her mind's eye but she pursued it, clinging on to every small detail that came to her. *Daylight was gone, the eve long commenced, with a pleasant breeze to cool the blood and dry the sheen of sweat upon her brow. Then came the awareness of dry heat still trapped and remembered in the red-brick wall under her left hand as she peeked around a corner looking to avoid the guard. The smell of wood smoke caught in her throat as she sidled behind the kitchens and stepped in a puddle of still-steaming, discarded vegetable water in a hollow between two cobbles. Then echoed the soft lilting curse of her accomplice as they nearly got accustomed by the sharp-boned Lady Dationna, yet were saved by a crash of porcelain as her maid acciden-tally dropped a tray behind her; and then – moments later: the sound of her own breath, sharp and rapid, as she and her accomplice beat feet down the long open gallery towards Klaas' chambers, all the while hoping that none of the other eight doors would open...*

With the crushing doom of exquisite antique cups and an irreplaceable blue and gold teapot ringing in her mind in line with the maid and Dationna's yelps of grief, Solancei flung her thoughts forwards, impatient...

The trouble, she feared, was that even when she'd laid eyes on 'said scroll', it hadn't exactly been in a full-blown study of the thing as much as it had been a hasty 'skim-through' of the highlighted points. Furthermore, she and her accomplice had found the instructions written, not in Common King's Tongue as expected, but in the poetic and somewhat complicated prose of ancient High Script: a language not used since the end of the Chaos Wars. *It was hard to translate; even harder to comprehend! And in a flash she recalled that feeling well-enough: the idea that this had been an ill-advised adventure to begin with: that Klaas was sure to find out; that this time she'd die from the punishment...*

Solancei shook herself, trying to keep a track of her place in the present even whilst the memories started to settle a little easier. Crammed together with the possibility of misinterpretation at the time, as well as the very vivid need to be in and out of Klaas' chambers before discovery put an end to the glorious foray, Solancei knew that even if she attained perfect recall of every word, she still might not have more than a haphazard guide to the template of success. She'd retracted deep: the Veranto was both a balm and an instrument, yet doubt continued to rile her in the form of unsavoury images and ideas that constantly collided with her intent, whispering of doom and of how she would never do this in time; under stress! *Gods but you cannot even remember the appropriate title of that scroll, can you? Soul Speech, was it? Or had it been Soul Reach?*

As if someone had snapped their fingers next to her ear, Solancei felt her precious Link beginning to falter a second time: the memories beginning to dry up; becoming less vivid. On a taunting whim, the picture of Zulavi somehow making off with Iambre burned itself into mind, followed by a picture of him towering before her friend and beckoning her to join him by accepting the marriage torque he was foisting on her. Like a bunch of starved vultures, other images followed, flocking to peck at her mind, killing her ability to focus on the set of instructions she'd laid eyes on, only once - and as she floundered, the starlight flared deep within her, as though in rage at her inability to perform when it mattered; as though it wanted her to pay attention and renounce this 'panic attack' for what it was! *And still, the archaic words of a scroll inked with blue, read in the faint light of one carefully shielded lantern, did not present them-*

selves in her mind's eye! All she remembered it seemed, were a scattering of words, a few interesting sentences taken out of context and made memorable only due to the construct of some unusual compositions like: 'softly as the wing of a dove' or 'searching beyond the call of bond'. Invaluable hints surely, yet on their own... useless!

Gods but she'd thought she could do this, but what if she couldn't?

A sensation akin to that of drowning in a sea of sudden, choppy waves, began to wash over her. Iambre was alone; she'd not be able to help; would not be able to make the necessary recall in time! Gods, but the scroll had been written in archaic times and it was a very plausible possibility that she and her friend might have translated entire paragraphs of text incorrectly due to nerves or simple lack of insight! Fleck, as a starting point, their entire translation had been based loosely upon Klaas' words anyway - well that, and their own fair knowledge, which at the time had been reluctantly drilled into them thrice a week by the royal master of letters – but...

Panic pulled at her, tearing her focus. *And dear Gods... just because she'd found High Script simple back then, it didn't necessarily mean that she'd learnt everything there was to know!*

Bloody swords, she recalled all too well just how, in her arrogance, she hadn't even bothered to practise as instructed. *Gods, why would she need to? It'd been a dead language. She'd never seen the future use, and now she was trying to bring back the image of something that must be at least eight years in the past!*

The cloying panic left her hollow with more self-doubt. The feelings came on so fast and so strong that she could not think or regulate her own breath quick enough to control it. Too much was happening. There was much too much at stake and too many twisted possibilities, which altogether made her capricious situation seem far too enormous to cope with!

But you must tell Klaas! You must get word to her! A voice of anger screamed inside - certain madness lurking in the crevices she glimpsed within herself. *Give in and-*

Before a score of other fears, her worries of burning herself out seemed selfishly pointless, and in the deep 'well' beyond her Link, the blazing light in her core seemed to flash with something akin to wrath: *seemed to flash and writhe, as it told her to reach! Reach towards it and... and see!*

But she couldn't. What she needed to see and what was on 'offer' were two different things and she could not accept. Not yet!

Solancei did not know how she did it but she pushed for one last finger-hold, then – wrenching her flighty attention back into line much like a commanding officer would a dozing soldier at an inspection. *'You will climb the stairs of the North Tower ten times!'* an echo of Klaas seemed to hiss in her ear; a memory... *'And don't you think about holding back again, girl. If you must run till you die, don't ever give in! Don't ever give in! And that's an order - do you hear! Don't give in... "*

Something awakened... something small but powerful. Something hot. Something with a root in anger! *Anger and training!*

Beyond the walls of her body, the traitor Zulavi was speaking again, but beat her if she could work it out any better this time.

He will never have Iambre, she promised herself. Simply. *Why are you still holding back when you know you can't afford to? Why?*

She could not answer, so she let go then; let her anger, and fear, and doubt, curl themselves around her core and mind as though they too were extensions of the Veranto: chasing shadows and doubts like cats chase mice!

There was only the Link. And the Recall. And there it was; suddenly: the stunted bit of knowledge she'd hoped to recover from the creases of her memory, the knowledge and odd bits of information that she somehow hoped was enough to extend her a moment of triumph. *And yes, blood fleck: it was called 'Soul Reach'!*

With one last flash of light from her core, calm rose up. *So much calm it seemed to be flooding her senses...*

She embraced it with a small sigh of gratitude. The sensation was literally 'peace'. It left a mental image behind: the surface of a still, dark forest lake returning to its former unbroken state of mirror-like perfection after the drops of a flash downpour had been swallowed.

And yet there was 'more'. Below that quiet surface, somehow tied to the ice and silver in her core, there were the anger and fear that fuelled her. The anger that still continued to sizzle, blackening the edges of her new serenity with its smouldering heat that no amount of calm, or water, or silvery light, could ever extinguish. But it was fine. Because now everything was contained behind a dam of clarity.

On one level she was aware that this was not classic Veranto; that the Enclave would probably never have condoned this bastardized use of the Art - but right at this moment, refinery was mote. There was nothing else to bolster her, nothing else to anchor her sanity and still retain enough courage to execute this, and though it raised her imaginary hackles to embrace the feeling, she stomped out the fear and allowed the hatred to burn until it shot white, ice-cold fire directly from her core through her veins.

It drained out the remainder of her feelings, suppressing everything, levelling – and then... *Crystal detachment rising beyond, yet still central, offering more than peace; more than breath...*

"The Crown Princess will never be yours." She spoke before she knew she was about to. The words from her mouth someone else's, yet intrinsically hers too.

With a chilled smile for the image constructing itself in her mind, more words followed. Words that mirrored truth and could saw through black glass with the simple purpose to warn.

"The Princess will never have you! She will never let you near!" Solancei floated somewhere in the anger and detachment near the surface of her body, but her awareness seemed to stretch, engulfing everything inside and out. As if someone else pulled the strings, she felt the smile widen as she nodded to herself, "Yes... yes, I think I understand... I understand now. Angemar was right: My Lord will die screaming. Like any other bastard-traitor. Like-"

Her words died. A sense of hectic shock was evaporating off the men and she let it reverberate in her core like a tonic to further numb her against fear and doubt, mentally and physically.

Not a trace of the New Wood accent remained now; only matter-of-fact words; words void of threat, hate or anger. Words of no return. Her carefully cultivated cover was forever ruined but she did not care.

Her mind felt free - like mentally, she'd already passed the final fork in the path to no recovery and the knowledge liberated.

"You wanted 'Truth', My Lord?" she whispered with a tint of disdain, unsure why she'd spoken again; unsure even if it was all simply in her head, or...

She swallowed, her mouth paper dry, her mind on fire as knowledge not her own stripped away her concept of self. With a smile for the things seen only 'in-between', she concluded, "Well... the truth is, My Lord, that the Enclave saw your 'illness', just as I see it now; they *saw* and they deemed you inept, and you know: the Enclave is never wrong. Such a poor fool not to understand that they will never revert their decision; that they cannot; and will not."

Though no mirth escaped the situation, she laughed quietly whilst she said something more – perhaps about the laws of the Enclave - but her words were becoming slewed as if she could not quite manage to concentrate enough to speak them properly. It made her sound Imkarahian and for half a heartbeat she wondered what the bastard would make of that. Honesty was her forte. In spite of what people like Palea might think, she did not deliberately go out of her way to insult others, but that was all applicable to someone else: to the life that beat within the shell of the body on the rack and she was far from this persona right now. *Far. Forgotten, even her name did not belong to her right then.*

A bright, frosty-tinged halo of light beckoned to break past the still surface of the imaginary pond but she held it back, the State of Veranto finally flowing like regular waves through her prone body, cancelling out everything...

"They'll dump you in the realm's deepest oubliette," she predicted, the slurring sounds forming almost incidentally, "And if they bother with a trial, you may have the chance to explain your actions, but I hear that the King is very, very fond of his daughter. I doubt me he will bother. Traitors just burn! And there's another truth! No matter what time in History you review, traitors climb the pyre."

It was like she was made of wind and ashes, suddenly; free from mind and body, she felt the distinct memory pressing now; calling now...

She didn't care if Simaro had listened or not. *'There is no way back now; no way out'-*, proclaimed a soft relentless voice she thought belonged to her body, *'-just keep running up those stairs! Keep running... find the strength... do your duty... run!'*

"I will stop you!" she promised the thin air on a soft breath, eyes already fixed on what only she could see. "I will stop you and I don't think there'll be a person left alive to piss on you out of kindness when those flames catch a hold!"

Solancei saw the wide lips in the pale face that belonged to her shackled body, part in a smile. It was both a feeling and a vision, then she was no longer there. Instead, remembering the exact feel of Klaas iron-bound main door opening without a sound to allow two clandestine shadows entry, she turned her attention to the past. *She'd almost also forgotten that her accomplice was a deft hand with the locks; the break-in had barely taken five breaths and she recalled thinking how annoyed Klaas would be if she knew how easy it'd been to gain entry...*

Like a feeling, her smile grew crooked: more than a memory. *She was without and within now – two halves; damnation and clarity... separating - and then she was riding in her own body once more – another time; another place...*

Somewhere without, she heard Zulavi gasp, comprehending perhaps that he might not sit with the winning hand after all, but the thoughts and feelings she'd experienced on that night eight years ago, were superimposing themselves over the present so that one seemed to cancel out the other. *She was clear on her task. Everything was utterly clear, even if it should perhaps not have been so.* Klaas had taught her to do one thing, but her duty to Iambre told her to do something else, whilst the Laws of the Enclave clearly stated that she must not go against any Master or else be penalised - but in this moment, regardless of how she played this, she'd be letting one or the other down and she was surprisingly candid about whose feelings mattered the most; indeed whose life! *Keep running...*

"You dare to think that you could stop me?! You think to waylay my plans?!" Zulavi's voice came from somewhere unknown. He sounded calm. *Had she even spoken aloud earlier?*

"Well try then, grey-eyes!" he invited with icy challenge, "Try, but I will shred you to pieces. The Enclave enjoys documenting these kinds of test and trials, no? Well, I shall make notes of your new journey for them to enjoy. And I shall give them your regards, of course; haunt them with the loss of their prodigy long after this realm becomes mine and my men tire of you! You can beg long and hard, and perhaps I might one day return them your broken flesh so they can study that too and view first-hand the errors they committed, but if not, know that the rift-fire and my Demonai are equally hungry!"

Though his softly menacing words should have had the power to make her mentally recoil, Solancei did not feel terror anymore. The part of her that was seeking out memories was too strong now. *Klaas chambers were dark... the smell of climbing wall-roses from without and the one kerosene lamp left burning within, somehow mingling into an odd scent that tickled her nose and sent her accomplice into a delicate fit of sneezes before containing it with a cotton pale handkerchief...*

"I will make you talk till your tongue bleeds, and you know-" Simaro's whisper seemed to float into her ear, along with the call of a hunting night hawk through the long narrow window the Chief had left open on a hasp to allow the night breeze to cool her rooms, "-it really gives me such great pleasure not to care a single whore's Mark - *silver or brass* - what happens to one of the Enclave's precious prodigies! Not a single Mark, grey-eyes! Now if that does that not smell like freedom, nothing ever will!"

Solancei waved a hand, dispelling with his voice as if it were a physical thing. She imagined she heard him speak something else, though it came to her through a veil of indifference: something... something about Angemar; and something about the Megaa'ron seeds, also known as the Red Haze on account of the poison turning the ensuing visions all shades of crimson.

They say it is an illusion of an adventure, too addictive to give up even if it proves as deadly as the bite of a viper-, she recalled Klaas saying, *-Gods, they say that to walk into the Red Haze is to give yourself over to another world: a world that only you can see; a world that will eventually kill you to be sure, but another world all the same; bliss, yet your worst nightmare! Don't you ever dare try this, girl! Don't you ever...*

"I will make you cry with regret and sorrow!" Zulavi promised, his voice somehow as unreal as the memory of Klaas' words and he was fading from her world once more.

In her heightened state she got the merest sense of warm breath against the curve of her ear... *as warm as the tentative breeze meandering in though Klaas' window... the roses smelled stronger than the oil lamp; she'd quite forgotten how lovely the scent of the night bloomers could be...*

The breeze became a hiss but from one breath to the next Simaro's ensuing words lost form. Time amalgamating out of place and space, her eyes swept – not across a dungeon ceiling, but through a door into the tidy functional space of the private office that belonged to her mentor. *Bookshelves to the left – featuring old tomes with faded silvered letters – some in red cracked leather binders, some wrapped in blue dust covers: the laws and judgements of the fifteen Provinces, recorded since the day of Unity. And to the right, the tall-backed heavy chairs standing sentinel along the wall upon which five ancient pennants hung as Klaas' personal reminder of the past...*

In the darkened room, her eyes still picked out the aged, faded splotches that marked the blood of fallen houses. These where the original five standards of her-

aldry recovered from the fields of the final battle of the Chaos War; in daylight, the
rust-coloured marks always gave her the chills, but-

"There it is!" her accomplice exclaimed with excitement, clapping both hands
together to make an annoying sound far too loud for this sort of venture and Solan-
cei startled, but only for a blink.

"Ouch!" Her friend's eager interest bumped Solancei physically against the
edge of Klaas' stout, but nicely carved dresser, simultaneously rattling the crystal
carafe perched atop and drawing the muffled sound from her as the other girl
pushed past her with a not-so-limber twist to skip through the open door of her
Mentor's private office. Rubbing her hipbone, Solancei followed her friend's direct
trajectory, her gaze skirting past the sombre ensemble of Klaas' dark furniture with
a measure of regret.

But her friend was right. Across the giant Iddian-pine worktable laden with
two stacks of documents to the left, and the slips of paper, ink and quill to the right,
lay the scroll of contention: all four foot of it fully unfurled as if it had been delib-
erately left out for them.

Solancei sucked in a breath.

Slowly, somehow fearing this a trap of some form, she crept forward, not quite
as trusting as her accomplice since she knew Klaas better than that. However, the
tightly woven rugs with their floral swirls and geometric central patters seemed to
hide the whisper of her footsteps as though in league with her purpose, and when
no guard stormed from the dark recesses to accost them, she finally threw caution
aside to hasten towards the sheltered lantern light how held high by her accomplice
so to better illuminate the scroll.

The anticipation was killing her, but she smiled. *She'd smiled back then too.*
In the world outside memory, Zulavi was going to ruin her. The least she could
do was to return the favour. So for Iambre, then...

Whispers From the Past

Nobody moved.

For the first time since the initial attack, Malandar suddenly sensed that the last remaining men might just keep their distance without encouragement and so whipped his attention towards the only remaining antagonist who still radiated hostile intent: *the one who'd cut him; the one he'd repelled.*

The cutthroat had hung back, allowing the First Guardian to take on his men, but perhaps not out of cowardice, because for all of the shock he must have experienced when the forces of magic hit him, this one seemed now more collected, more assiduous even, than any of his comrades.

It made the First Guardian assume that the criminal must be the group's leader even before he spotted the golden pin upon the man's surprisingly well-made arming doublet. Its presence combined both the man's captaincy as well as that of his love for Silicia'Cha, and Malandar felt his own power shimmer instantly in response to this open display of misguided fealty.

Still, no matter what had come before, the captain was nothing if not careful now as he approached with sure readiness to wield both a sword and a long-bladed parrying dagger.

With no words spoken, all sound seemed to drop from reality, yet somehow their leader's unfaltering display of courage did not appear to cheer the remaining gang members. Where action had created moments of chaos only heartbeats earlier, his people now remained utterly still as they continued to watch the odd display of conflict from their vantage point at the periphery of proceedings.

Malandar did not waste his attention on their change, or would-be, lack of heart. The captain's smug confidence was washing over him in a way he could not ignore: like a dark patch of clouds rolling in on strong winds to kill a bright afternoon.

It seemed an overall odd contrast to the leader's otherwise quiet behaviour and it was hence almost disconcerting when the man began to smile – his ribald stare continuous and unbroken: tagged by equal measures of poisonous disdain and vulgar intent.

In response, Malandar's Guardian instincts hummed strangely as a familiar vibe went through his runes, intensifying exponentially suddenly when the captain paused mid-step, still paces shy of engaging.

Strangeness permeating the atmosphere like the scent of imminent rainfall, the two men studied one another silently for a beat. Then, like some peculiar near-sighted lizard, the would-be thief and killer cocked his head in a slightly odd manner to peer at the First Guardian: his bearded chin tilting first this way, then the other, quite as if his slow appraisal did not allow him the use of all his faculties though he looked fully hale to the eye.

"You look different... yes..." the man said pensively after a few hesitant beats, "You disguise much but indeed I see that you are 'he', are you not? *You... Are... He...*"

As if to punctuate his strange statement, the man issued a peculiar shrill sound, unexpectedly affecting something in-between laughter and mockery. Then, with a coquettish glint belonging in the eye of a promiscuous woman rather than a burly man, he tittered with something best termed 'insincere re-gret'.

Obscure reasoning carrying the sudden stench of personal delight, yet permeated slightly by what felt to Malandar like a slice of habitual sarcasm, the other man ventured, "But so it's true then. And well-well, so we start over, but my... how I am surprised! Oh my–my indeed..."

The words rode into the First Guardian, stroking to life a sense of recognition - and again he saw a hint of deft appraisal flickering in the man's gaze.

With a smile, the rogue captain half-sang, half-spoke, "But how 'Human' you look Gu'ardian; so... *so dreadfully ordinary... so... so easily tamed...* it must...

"Yes, it must be those baby-fawn eyes you've veiled the truth behind - they work very well: I confess I was nearly fooled by the simplicity, yes - but I see, Gu'ardian. Oh yes, do I see because your magic still burns. And so I see you. And you are 'he'!"

Gu'ardian... That particular infliction was just right, but it couldn't be, could it?

As though in answer, a glacial hatred fluttered to life deep within Malandar. It seemed impossible, but the curiously lilting whisper, along with the not-entirely wholesome thing Malandar had already spied in the depths of the captain's deep eyes, struck a chord.

Yet ever-prepared, he hadn't expected this; ever-prepared, for a moment he could only gaze at the captain in what felt to him, as close to surprise as he'd been in a long while. *The Captain? Silicia'Cha be damned: a Vessel? Her Vessel? Here? But surely not...?!*

"And by my Brothers and Sisters," the other man whispered like a viper slowly undulating across silk, now issuing another low chuckle laced with part-derision, part-admiration, "Oh, but I think I had quite forgotten me how magnificent you are, my Elvern *Mal'Nahvar.* I'd... I'd forgotten how delightfully delicious! But come now, My Dark Breath, you should visit me soon! You should come see me beyond this tedious realm upon which you walk with such stealth to ignore its reeking, small Humans and the stench of decaying magic. Come to me. Come."

Wrath fanning a little deeper, Malandar blinked slowly. If he hadn't, he might have physically recoiled from the hateful creature's invite.

"Oh but I am so bored,-" the man's tone became a sultry sulk, "-Gu'ardian, I am so unpleasantly bored – there is nothing here to entertain us - but come to me; delight this Goddess in her halls of spun illusion and ancient dust! If you prove charming, I would even let you leave again; you are my favourite of the ten-"

Silicia'Cha halted mid-sentence, a sublime show of simulated shame stretching her Vessel's mouth in a pretence of abashed apology to have blundered so carelessly.

"Ups..." Eyes growing wide in rotten innocence, the man emitted a short giggle, then composed himself on a breath, proving beyond a doubt that the sentiment could not have been less sincere as he hiccupped with embarrassment. "Ups, slip of the tongue there – I meant: my favourite of *the nine,* of course."

A teasing silvery peal of laughter echoed on a breath - imagined, not real - not issuing from the captain but travelling on the air. It raised Malandar's hackles...

"But so silent you are my Mal'Nahvar. Am I not pleasant? Do I not speak with eloquence and grace? Am I not just as worthy of your interest as our dear, maimed Ulvaro'Cha?" The captain shook his head in mock sadness, then looked Malandar boldly in the eye. "Oh, but how you scarred her. Remember? She hates you so, you know. But when you come I will not tell her – she would insist on taking what you owe her from that fair skin of your backside – but it would not work now, would it? The hag would only be swopping one damaged hide for another, wouldn't she, and so then she might take your flesh from the bones instead, and I would so hate that, Gu'ardian. See that is not what I want from you – not unless you give it to me freely, and out of love, of course..."

The man issued another cackle – a sound that should not have belonged in his mouth - and for a blink the First Guardian felt transported into some strange twisted illusion of reality, barely ready to believe his own eyes as he stared into those of the Goddess' lurking beneath the man's. The taunting words that turned his stomach were grotesquely at odds with the rough appearance of the guy before him - and hence the reason he could not be wrong, yet still...

There was no doubt the captain before him was a Vessel, but black Fell! Why hadn't he felt it?

Narrowing his gaze he conceded it didn't matter now. His given heritage responded to the verification with another blast of cool wrath that made his runes burn with a need to annihilate. It took effort, but he controlled the hard urge to lash out with the magic and with a bitter twist for the need, started forward instead, sword at the ready.

As he might have predicted, it was what the Goddess' Vessel had expected.

With a hiss of warning, stained yellow teeth barring, Silicia'Cha's pawn flung himself forward too: as though driven by a secret signal, raising weapons as if in readiness to kill, though the Goddess would already be aware of the futility. Still, She was like a bored petulant child and She wanted him to lash out with the magic - *perhaps to spend himself further, perhaps for simple amusement* – and Malandar's instinct to release a Weave of Destruction was rekindled in a blink as he faced the creature she controlled.

If he obliged though, in a manner of speaking, She would have controlled him too, and if the idea of sending her back to Her lair howling in pain seemed tempting beyond measure, he resisted. *He'd already done quite enough with that first Weave to irrefutably confirm his return to the Realms; She didn't need another display to know this for certain; he didn't need to waste the power...*

As though driven by a rogue spell to do so, Malandar angled Heruvar, battering away the enemy blades as the attack hit him. In response, a feast of feelings rolled within the Goddess' eyes in just one blink: lust, envy, triumph, regret, humour, want, hatred, demand, incredulity!

It meant nothing; like an extension of his mind and purpose, he swung the sword...

Cleaving the air with the sharpness of a direct moonbeam, humming its soft mystic tune as if born of an elemental spirit, the smoothly beautiful steel rushed forth like a single eye-piercing flash of liquid lightning, shattering parts of her witchcraft but not all. *It was a promise to the Maker; a guarantee of demise and it stayed the trajectory, travelling up and around in an unwavering blur that made contact inevitable...*

As if he knew his fate but aimed to mock, the Vessel's feral smile became wider then, almost in a sickening parody of amusement as he attempted to sidle around and bring his own weapons into play, but it did not affect the outcome. Heruvar drew across the captain's neck right below the jaw, biting deep like the knife of a slighted Ermaron mistress to strike the man's head cleanly from the body with enough purpose to launch it sideways like a boulder released from the basket of a ballista. *Done...*

An echo of something more sinister than plain female fury seemed to linger in the First Guardian's mind for a blink - then it was gone, washed away as the man - whose headless bulk now folded with an almost graceful ripple – proceeded to topple as though his insides had liquidized.

The Vessel had not been the first one deluded by his faith in Silicia'Cha and fooled by the act of free will to be subjugated. This man had made the mistake of believing himself better protected than any of his newly deceased or dying comrades and as the severed head cut a perky course, it still bore an expression of dumb surprise.

It was not an uncommon look for a Vessel, Malandar recalled without pleasure as he stepped clear of the headless bulk just before the spreading puddle of blood could make contact with the toe of his right boot; the subtle leather was as dark as charcoal, almost black, and the man's life fluid would likely as not show upon the treated hide, but that was not the point.

Come visit me...

Malandar grimaced as cool revulsion rolled along his runes.

"I will visit you Khi'nesta, only when I come with the purpose to kill!" he mumbled under his breath, rescinding her repulsive invite out of sheer contempt, barely sparing the master-less head a glance before turning then to gauge the mould of the remaining perpetrators.

He needn't have bothered.

They did not roost to rush him, nor did they rush to escape. In fact, rather than move, the 'show' appeared to have rooted them without even the slightest use of magic - and as they stood there, utterly transfixed by their captain's head, their silent mesmerised fascination matched their pale-faced horror hand-in-glove.

Recognising the symptoms of shock, Malandar bit back a wholesome Venzoian curse. This was exactly the sort of impracticality that befell people without fail when something 'impossible' happened. It preceded a state of true terror that always set in like a perfect bell, just around the time they regained enough wherewithal to imagine they'd probably be next for similar treatment, and off it went...

Again, as per experience, it was a fairly standard reaction and the First Guardian wondered if these men would prove the kind to break and bolt, or the type to find heart and seek retribution?

Not understanding what made him think of the next thing, but nevertheless well within the brackets of 'strange' already experienced on this day, he almost snorted in amusement. *Had Richarmarlan Envalair been present, wagers to the exact time and effect would've been coerced from him... and anyone else present. Yet now, however...*

Dispelling with stray memories, derision floated, then drowned. Until he knew the minds of these insects, their fate hung in the balance and Malandar held back - the men's sustained lack of aggression now tying his next step as surely as a verbal command from Alérathnar Himself-

The head made impact. The accompanying, but resounding, moist 'thud', weighed heavily on the senses as it bounced, somersaulting just once, to cover the remaining short distance towards its unwilling 'audience'.

Like everything else, it struck Malandar wrong for some reason, and he watched the men carefully, their apathy too involved. Which was odd. *For an attack lead by a Vessel, there was something not quite right. Something...*

Losing its inertia, the macabre ball rolled the last few yards like an old leather sack stuffed with rubble before reaching its final pose, from whence it settled an accusing glare at the three men.

The 'event' seemed to shake-up the flat-nosed man in the ragged blue tunic and scarf on the far right. With a slight wobble, he heaved. Then swallowing hard and sucking-down multiple, rapid breaths, he heaved again – the two curved long-knives in his now limp hands no longer a threat as his pose crumbled further and all previous strength seemed to leech from his person as though pulled and neutralised by a nefarious spell.

It happened too fast.

In the time it would take a dancer to clap her hands once, reality had shown its face and then 'squash-nose' turned pasty, a blink later emptying his guts with a gushing, vehement sound. Spinning from the sight of death, narrowly preventing himself from despoiling his former leader, the sick man showed a strange rise in decency that took the First Guardian aback. This was not the reaction of a hardened killer, and certainly not that of a mind-meltingly stupid 'Elated' either. This... this was something other...

A subtle stench of bile rising and wafting through the air, Malandar crinkled his nose, not from refined detest – *though the Maker knew there was a hint of that!* - but from ill-concern. A sliver of alarm slithered like a swamp adder down his back, a rare thing indeed, and not right for the effect. His spirit seemed to have stilled; the runes were quiet...

Feeling an unwilling spectator to a freakishly odd performance similar to those so favoured by his father's people due to the unpredictable twists and developments in the drama, Malandar knew a moment of unsettled spirits. Unlike flat-nose, the other two men never blinked, though the one in the middle – a fair-haired, weak-chinned guy with a scar on his cheek – heaved just once too, as though in response to the witnessed misery. Concentrating more on the head, however, both he and the young lad on the left had eyes as big as fat toads.

It put Malandar in mind of a pair of over-zealous First Tier apprentices that hoped to Persuade a Weave of suitable character to make the head go 'poof - but with little result.

Black fell... poof? In spite himself the First Guardian felt his lips quiver.

Morbid mirth. In these times, also not right! Indeed, so very much not right that the 'good' Marlan Envalair would have wondered if Malandar Denarlin's precious head had received damage somehow, before laughing hard at the possibility of the First Guardian ever lapsing from his perch of punishing discipline.

Malandar exhaled, the harsh reality sobering, the sense of blackened humour evaporating. *Marlan... laughing...*

Incidentally, with a bit of magic, the rider-less head might very well have evaporated, but Malandar did not think these the men of sufficient discipline, even had they had the Affinity or – curse it all – the flows, to Persuade into an appropriate spell. *Still... as he'd noted before, this was most assuredly not the behaviour of men devoted to Silicia'Cha – nor any other deity for that matter! In fact, now that the Vessel was gone-*

A panicky moan escaped the man on the far right as he broke from sicking-up to stumble as though he were about to faint, yet somehow succeeded in catching himself enough will to prevent the indignation. Unsteady on his feet, his colour could rival that of a corpse, though...

Malandar was waiting for sanction – but Alérathnar did not grant it as expected; did not release the First Guardian to move. *Why?*

He could hear the heavy breaths of the survivors' rising fear; if he tried hard he might even have been able to hear their racing hearts, but he had no reason to. In truth, had he thrown a spell to simulate, the First Guardian knew he could not have managed a better, more pointless stalemate. *Now what was he to do with them? What?*

It was an uncalculated nuisance that brought with it its own problems and though his senses already bathed in returning peace, strangely enough, his first thought was not of relief or triumph, but rather of Guardian Envalair again. Almost, he imagined he could see the dead Guardian's ghostly applaud and hear the faded press of Marlan's dry humour vibrate from his core. Almost he could...

'My... but well done,' the dead Guardian seemed to congratulate him in whispered tones of good-will sarcasm that were of course nothing but a figment

of memory, *'Well done indeed, Sakarai Regichi! But now? Tell me, how would you End it?'*

Malandar blinked to rid himself of the uncomfortable sensation of his old friend breathing in his ear and the spectral illusion began to fade, though not without leaving an echo of Guardian Envalair's final words to drift like the end-tail of a severed Weave, *'So you do know, of course, what you must do - but will you do what you must, Sakarai Regichi? Would you? Will you?'*

Out of the quiet evening, another weak groan of fear spliced the atmosphere, thereby releasing the imagined and bringing Malandar's reality harshly back into focus; Richarmarlan Envalair was long dead, Malandar's own weary mind simply playing a game of smoke and mirrors. He was surrounded by death and the dying, by fear and blood. That was real!

However, if 'the voice' in his mind was but a painful wraith of days long gone, it still spoke the truth.

For what would he do? What... Sakarai Regichi?

The sizable problem of this double-edged question was not lost on him but neither was the reoccurring lack of choices - and to 'hear' the spectre call him by an old nickname as if their world had not changed a dozen times over...?

Vexed that he should experience distraction, the reference to the old days disturbed, and though not experienced for longer than many would name 'an eternity', Malandar found a sudden simple want to embrace old instincts that welled to life within his core: no cost, no thought for oaths or pacts – just freedom.

A coldness of winter's depth crept forth, beckoning, breaking the Guardian restraint that held him back. His clarity rarely failed, but this ancient feeling brought to life the remembered promise of absolution through violence; it guaranteed instant gratification through the link to his shunned heritage, and then-

Of course, the unending frost was of a kind the Maker could not allow him to embrace – yet in this very moment, as Malandar stood here amidst the stench of pollution and guts, tangy blood and vibrating magic, he suddenly strained to recall why that should rule him. *The Maker had bound him but he could still negate his oaths regardless. Because it would be easier...*

Again the artless, ferocious simplicity of another life, *another time*, pulled - the purpose clean and unembellished. *He needed to silence these men... and he could. He should.*

It was an odd truth that found him venturing one menacing step towards the still-mesmerised men before he knew the stab of warning down the runes. *This would not be sanctioned. Alérathnar would not allow this...*

Malandar halted as though controlled by iron wires.

The aggressive movement had caught the attention of the two closest renegades, however, and as awareness snapped its jaws, alerting to the lingering danger, he both felt and saw the moment the head on the ground became the sudden secondary terror.

'But why do you stop now, Sakarai Regichi?' Richarmarlan's dead voice seemed to rasp in his ear - a menacing taunt he barely recognized as one belonging to his dead Guardian friend, and yet an unmistakable reminder of the words Marlan had once ventured in anger on a day so very long ago now; on the day before they sealed their fate to the Maker's cause; on the day they'd both still been alive, fuelled by fury, angered by loss; exhausted, spent, hurting...

Desperately hunting a way out; a way forward; a way to preserve what was left of the realms and of what they knew; what they loved – there'd been little either of them could do to protect the right of all life, except perhaps for one thing...

'Risk it! Don't risk it! Just run the risk!' the echo carried on, *'Yet you will not, but you must Malandar – or all will fail! Belingarn Well is burning, Nefer'soeryn is enslaved, the Plains of Ra'fyn-narah buckles under the footfall of their advance to the south and shrivels north and west with the traps of a hundred Neidar'barai! Some hope King Zosarh will reach us in time; we know he will not! This is the last stand, and you can no longer afford principles, nor can you afford to fear what will be if you cannot control yourself! Heliandrai is gone! In hours, all will be gone! Do this, I beg you, and your Uncle will come; he has no choice – you will draw him forth! Flesh and burning skies friend, if not this, what would you do instead? What?!'*

In Malandar a dark impatience welled up, a dread flinching through muscles and bones, laying siege to the Guardian. Clenching his teeth till his jaw ached from the strain, he knew the sense of wrong enhancing, the vibrating tension in his core never one that should transfer to the runes on his skin, nor the

picture of the world before his eyes. Yet the argument to embrace the destructive path some part of him suddenly craved, spread like the essence of existence
itself.

'Do this and we have a chance...'

The vibration became a quiver, silver light rising, sending a soft tremor
through the fingers of his sword hand. Detachment widening, like a chasm
slowly birthed by the shifting, opposing forces of primordial geology, he felt
the ancient, but ever-denied 'Shape Caster' stir within his own skin. *He hadn't
relented when it mattered the most – Marlan hadn't understood that Malandar
couldn't do so even when compelled by a skies painted black and crimson by fire and
magic, and with the defiant haunting screams of the last men on the front standing against Chaos. But if he finally gave in, perhaps the guardian discipline might
serve where nothing but gaping oblivion had previously threatened. It was the closest he'd come in a long while to daring, and-*

The clash of the old raked up the ashes burying still-smouldering embers
under the Maker's Oath, and suddenly the line of reason seemed oddly paper-
thin and ready to combust if he only allowed it. He was tired of the fight, he
realised. *Perhaps too tired...*

Overlaying the soft tremor in his hand, the familiar Ink of Power was slowly
staining the tips of his fingers, a liquid arising like a backwards trail up past
his nails, past the joints of his distal phalanx - permeating like a pest, requiring
none of the Maker's power nor the Ostravahn flows, and proving that whatever
Guardian Mehand'Arun might claim, he did still own personal choice.

'Why do you stop...? Heliandrai is gone...'

Malandar pushed the memory aside before the fey promises of a heritage-
denied could un-stitch his hold on the present. *Damnation... what the fleck was
happening to him?*

Stealing another breath, this one heavy from the control he sought to re-
assert, he slowly rolled his eyes from the man in the middle who couldn't seem
to fathom why the three of them yet lived, though the fortune of each breath
was an explosion in his chest to confirm it so. Like a tune in the air set below
human hearing, Malandar was aware as the man wobbled on the spot, hatchet
and short-sword quivering in white-knuckled hands. *The sorry wretch might yet
begin to pray. The Human had the look of a prayer monger...*

Agitated that he was, as First Guardian, Malandar sincerely hoped the renegade would refrain, though. Prayers might yet serve to shift this unchecked horror within him past care, and even a prayer to the Mad Ones would not be enough to sanction more death. *Alérathnar's Runes had gone quiet; the First Guardian's authority to react without mercy had definitely been revoked.*

Malandar Denarlin Cor'Esardan rarely felt like swearing, yet incredibly, the urge was there right then - as if by exclaiming every crude Slave or Venzoian word known to him, he could somehow stamp down on everything that was out of place!

There was 'heritage'. And then 'Heritage'. 'The spectre' had been right. Perhaps it was time to risk it all. Only this time...

Malandar breathed-in, one long steady pull of heavy air.

Razing his eyes over the three men – one final time searching for Silicia'Cha's touch and daring them to move, daring *Her* to send forth just one tiny waft of rancid 'perfume', he weakly tried to figure out why he should still feel like exterminating them? *For the offence of having held back when their comrades rushed him? For the slight against his Guardian title? For ignorance? To keep the path tidy?*

Malandar grimaced, the sense of morbid humour striking twice. He had never been that fickle, but now he wished he were. *Marlan would've found a way, but...*

Try as he might, the First Guardian could no longer find any resonance of the Goddess' madness within any of them; She could not have 'marked' them, there was no lingering hostility towards him. Instead, he simply felt two sets of petrified eyes suddenly riveted to his person with the level of intensity people usually reserved for their first sighting of a wild predator or a hunting Venzoian. *Unbelievably, flat-nose on the right was retching again. Softly now. Eyes glazing with denial. Again a reminder...*

Incidental concern flaring as his self-control compacted, yet expanded, Malandar felt the ferocious flood finally retract, ceding room for reason and thought once more.

'*Oh, but why did you stop, Sakarai Regichi?*' Marlan's incorporeal voice lamented – an echo of an echo, '*They made a choice, did they not? They sided with Chaos. They know what they deserve but now...? What will you do, now?*'

The silent words cementing his dilemma, a crooked frown pulled at his brows. *Yes, what exactly would he do? About this? About everything?*

Ancient Manuscript

SOLANCEI SHIFTED. Or maybe she did not? For a curious moment, she felt ancient. Then not.

But the old scroll with the faded blue ink lays unrolled before her eyes, yet again – pretty once, she imagines – but the gilded border is flaking, all but gone in some places as though rubbed from existence by a hundred set of hands all exploring the same section of text over and over. The wear does not detract, however, it simply makes it valuable and the ornate capital letters entwined in pictures that preside over each new paragraph, are tiny works of art, even if they are barely embossed anymore. She does not find it hard to imagine the once-glittering show of colour either: red, green and blue – but sadly they are but a faded imitation of former glory. Such is time, she thinks: it both erases and polishes.

She lifts the lantern from her accomplice's hand, then opens two more shutters to emit a warm pool of candlelight and the shallow indentations of the print gleams in sullen response. Her small action makes it only three shutters out of six but their eyes are young and she daren't open the lantern completely for fear that someone might see the gleam from without and alert the Chief of the 'activity'.

The thought of that makes her shiver, for Gods know, she should not be here; but then she corrects herself for she is not alone, and neither of them should be here! If they are found out...

But reason dictates they will not be caught now – or so she flecking hopes! Klaas is in a council meeting but who knows when the Chief might return. There is never a set time to these things: this foray must be done quickly; sooner rather than later, lest they get into trouble. Lots, and heaps, of epic trouble...

And yet she is not here to make mischief; she tells herself that she's come to Klaas' chambers tonight out of necessity, for this is a 'quest' for knowledge that would otherwise be denied her for many more years – maybe forever if her skills do not bear the fruit of her promise - and there is a genuine interest behind her ill-advised adventure even if it is not sanctioned, and as for her companion...

She glances at her 'accomplice' and knows the other girl's interest a little simpler than her own. Her companion is not fortunate enough to carry the spark within to Link herself with the State of Veranto, but she shares Solancei's quaint interest in all things historic and this scroll is definitely one for them both! She observes her short, pale-haired companion with surreptitious fascination as the unlikely friend bends in for a closer look: instantly mouthing ancient words under her breath as she reads to herself.

Her accomplice has a voice that could melt ice. Her short stature is easily compensated by her 'presence' and of course those big blue eyes of hers: eyes that sparkle with excitement now; eyes set above a freckled nose of such flecking cute perfection that even Iambre cannot compete.

As expected, her companion doesn't appear to note Solancei's soft scrutiny as she peruses the text in apt fascination. It seems she is better at concentrating than Solancei right now, a fact Lancei will not let stand and so she too bends closer, abandoning quaint observation for later.

Fascination flares instantly. It's like the text wants to be read. They try not to touch the scroll as they skim the contents, quick to recover from surprise that is in fact written in the old prose. It seems too much a transgression to mar the old parchment with yet more fingers than it has already suffered through the ages but the words within are all very poetic – something neither of them had realised from the snippets the Chief read aloud earlier.

But perhaps Klaas did not bother to include the finer points?

It makes sense, Lancei accedes to herself: the Chief did probably not wish to give away enough information that it might accidentally tempt misuse – ironic it seems, since the very lack of detail is what finds them here now...

Feeling the cut of her own sabre-sharp reasoning, she offers the room a grimacing apology, yet keen to waste no time, Lancei still bends closer, catching the dry mellow scent of antiquity riding in the presence of the scroll.

The smell calms her but throughout, she carries a heightened awareness of time. It seems forever before they reach the first bullet made out in old numerals with a crane wrapped around the outer edge on the left, fashioned as to be part of the number, its pointy beak striking over the top and down in an artistically pleasing manner that lends the picture flow and balance.

"Point one:-" her accomplice reads aloud, squinting in the poor light, for a moment withholding a breath as if tethering on an edge.

Solancei reins back impatience but gives her a nudge.

For a scroll that may not see much daylight, the parchment is pliable and stays flat against the table without rolling – in fact, it looks almost like soft hide before it is treated and turned into vellum – but her accomplice denies the possibility without room for discussion, and she knows

the other girl feels nervous then, from the way she continues to pet the curling end of that thick,

blonde plait she hooks over her left collarbone as though it were a pet snake.

"Point one:-"the girl repeats. Captivated and seemingly lost in her own passion, she reads on, "-'Catalessa impredsanho dosea marquite et durales immessa travihonta ai, noi presontur calmarai motivartes Novissariar ni Abiliaiar?"

Eyes unfixing from the text, she looks away in thought, gently performing a preoccupied staccato tap with one finger against the edge of the table as she appears to consider the words. With a vexed sigh, she bestows Solancei a frown, honing in on her face with her near-sighted squint.

"So, 'Catalessa'... Sleep? So Sleep Will Obtain...? Obtain what? Obtain Calm? No. Steadiness, perhaps? No-'

"No Heneia," Solancei interrupts, slightly annoyed that her 'accomplice' is not seeing the obvious, yet somehow managing to cut back on attitude, "No: Catalessa translates as: 'trance', not sleep... and..."

She pauses and they both fall silent whilst Lancei does a quick skim of the entire paragraph - just to be sure...

Haltingly, she proceeds to formulate into words what is already swirling in her mind, the translation not yet entirely solid but speaking aloud, the soft sound of her own voice somehow helps her place the words in the right order, "No, this is written like poetry, remember? Each paragraph will sound like a stanza. And in the style of Chaos Wars writing, it's semi-back-to-front.

"So this is not 'Point One', but... but, '1st signifier', and then... then: 'Trance is'... 'is accomplished slowly through the'... 'the need'? No... not 'the need'; maybe, 'a

need'? Or is it just 'Need'? Yes, through 'Need and'... 'and emerges'? No... no, 'sub-merges the mind in'... 'in calm, not to be attempted by'-"

"-By Apprentices or Adepts." her accomplice completes the sentence with a tri-umphant smirk and looks up from the faded text at the same time as Solancei. Heneia's blue eyes seem guileless in the dim light but Lancei reads the message in their glittering depths regardless: 'You are only an apprentice, perhaps we ought to leave it'?

She shakes her head - an action that somehow links her present with the past: she is no longer an apprentice! And as if it mirrors that which once happened, Heneia catches Lancei's smile with a scheming one of her own – her blue eyes shrewd with the intrigue of their bold illicit outing as she slowly nods in agreement across the stretch of vellum.

They are in accord. This is an old document; they may never get the chance again.

"2ⁿᵈ Signifier,-" her blue-eyed accomplice grins in open delight, showing dim-ples, as their conjoined attention ducks back down to the scroll like a pair of swoop-ing birds of prey to decipher the next paragraph,"-Recorporales inorgentalar hav-istes calmarai terron nachtorai giventes poidrama noi-..." the old words are writ-ing themselves across Lancei's mind now; the memory flowing fast and smooth-ly like the River Kekarnarah in spring.

How could she ever have thought that she might not recall? The icy fear of discovery still rides along her shoulder blades, making her tighter than last years' boots: she had trespassed in Klaas chambers back then, and it felt like she was trespassing yet again; stepping onto ground best-forgotten, toying with skills best left alone for she has no training, no experience, except...

Except, that was then – and this is now! And in the years in-between, Klaas had taught her well, hadn't she!?

Of course, had Solancei been face to face with Klaas right this moment, her mentor would still tell her not to do this; would still try to dissuade her because she hadn't had any previous experience, but Klaas was not here to stop her - just as she hadn't been in that room all those years ago – and in a flash of higher insight, Solancei suddenly knew that she could do this. The State of Veranto seemed to fit her purpose, hand-in-glove. This was the best she'd ever been: for-gotten information now blooming once more in her head, the details complex like something woven in a dream, and thereby offering the insight sought all along.

A detached sense of bliss rode back in to envelop her. *She and her Accomplice are reading in sync now, grinning like excited school girls because they've almost gotten away with this; grinning because this is a magnificent bit of learning: secrets they are not supposed to know the particulars of, and yet here they are...*

"*The 9th and final Signifier then*," *the two of them half-whisper, half-speak, in unison.* "*Retrovarai numeratica toi, delforlatai vrai destrai; delantas poi ellemelem toi; respirrai tolma velosakrah korsakraai. Toi emotatasai emoriertu vetzalai vrai.*"

It translated, 'And thus you will re-discover the right path, as the reality recounted passes forth to lead you back to the elemental point of desire within time and breath. However, stand wary of true failure for it will bring the Beyond without regard'.

"*Moy devalantes vrai stargenzu erkerez cel Vizzavaltir toi kapsolrai vente. Portervrainu beganurah Animartu mortaron poi. Melyra legetziar nar dom deviansa.*"

'And the trick is not to go deep but to culture your distance: to pick your moment of connection, to return to it by Will and Search until you find the Deviant. Beware thus that your Will be centred or the Soul Reach will not transcend into life. Look for the Moment Out of Time. Where necessary, the Master might choose to avail themselves of the Long Breath...'.

As Solancei witnesses it all unfold, she never doubts the translations, and suddenly she does not doubt them now either. She notices the exact point when her accomplice looks up at her in awe; this is before they fall out - before betrayal kills their odd friendship - and as of yet feelings are not marred.

"*Lancei... this is big!*" *her friend breathes, keeping Solancei pinned with her summer-sky blue eyes just a heartbeat longer before she looks back down on the text as if she is trying to take everything in one more time.*

"*And you think you will know how to do this?*" *her companion enquires, the same awe still there in her full, velvet voice.*

Solancei shakes her head; a little overwhelmed; like Heneia, a little in awe of what they have just learnt.

"No... no, I've not a clue how I'd even start,-" she admits wryly, the fogs of the past hiding true comprehension, *"-not even the slightest clue, Heneia. But one day... one day I will!"*

And now she does. In fact, now she knows exactly where to begin; now she understands just how to forge the necessarily Link.

And so she is relieved to see through new eyes that it is mostly a matter of discipline; a matter of choosing the right moment in time - the right conditions. It is something she could not have comprehended eight years ago when she was still only an Adept, but now she understands the theory. And she must do this. She can do this!

Solancei distanced herself but imagined a smile cruising her lips though she wasn't sure if it was made physical or if it remained simply a feeling. But what did it matter? When once asked if the subject of the scroll could really do as described, Klaas had sniffed, then told her 'yes'. Klaas would have had no reason to lie – not with Enclave 'magic' - and besides, Solancei needs to believe now! She had to make this work! *And there was a day... a day...*

Time blurred as she stepped from Klaas' chambers like a Dream Walker, rushing towards a point that was almost steady in her mind. *It was a particular day she searched for. A day... not too long ago, where monotony had ruled. She remembers it well because of that ruddy dog – and so this day should serve her most perfectly to forge the necessary 'Moment out of Time'.*

"Knights Commander,-" she murmured, partly lost in the past, partly reaching for the future, though she was also aware of a body locked in the present, "-do your worst. Do your best. Meer'ron or not... you will burn."

As if someone else possessed the ability to formulate the words that came, she could not feel her mouth move or her thoughts form into the simple warning, but the stab of satisfaction she felt was not unpleasant.

"You see, there's this skill... a skill amongst the Masters: an Event known to us as 'Soul Reach'; an Event that allows two Masters to join together in awareness and presence through the State of Veranto, and I think... well, I imagine, your trial will not be long... after... this."

"Black pox, there is no such thing! You lie!" Zulavi's denial of the truth was a violent sound in her ear. She ignored it and his displeasure became the growl of an angered predator prowling another world as he repeated, "You lie!"

She still did not bother to respond. *She was done with him.* Perhaps she smiled again, the notion of sweet vindication sauntering through her, but maybe she only imagined it. From somewhere far away, she heard the string of heated demands that followed but though the emotions seemed strangely tangible, she no longer needed to listen nor fear him. The calm she was familiar with - now permeating her completely - seemed to keep everything at arm's length. She felt ethereal. *This was the edge of Veranto just as she'd known it before the headaches and the glitches: this was perfection, and this... this...*

Already the horizon seemed to burn in her mind's eye, the heat rising up off the day she'd sought, shimmering across her vision in ripples of distortion. *Now... to find that Moment...*

Something locked onto her upper arms then – *shaking her?* - but it did not alter anything; it did not affect her. Her body was without, her work within – two separate entities - and his petty anger could not reach her in the place she was going.

...And there was a day, not long ago, where monotony had ruled and she'd been unhorsed and plonked unceremoniously onto her arse because of that flecking dog, yes...

Sinking into the memory as though she was melting into a daydream, she soon brought up the feel and the smells as she remembered them surrounding her that day and after she'd practised recalling the words of the scroll, this was not hard.

Hot, arid, sunny, hot... she'd placed the relevant scene into context within a blink and without a hitch. The movements of land and weather followed, cementing into sync with the day's trivial events: the relentless travelling that saw well over three-hundred and fifty people moving no quicker than a walking child; the creaking spokes of the supply vehicles protesting against the abuse of hidden hollows and raised patches of ground the size of molehills; the punishing jolts that would shake the larger wagons when they hit either of the above; mounted soldiers muttering curses under their breath when horses misstepped or got spooked by hissing lizards or rearing vipers; the mad whinny of a horse stung by a hornet; Iambre's lacquered carriage playing arrow-head to the line of vehicles that followed, its smart design so evidently out of place that the Princess would have been better served walking, for progress was slow and laborious and hazardous.

In grotesque opposition to the general feel of the people and animals surrounding her, the black and green streamers and the leopard banners of the royal house had been whipping cheerfully in the breeze all morning - up until an hour ago. Then the wind had died and the knowledge that everyone suffering this route simply because of the Princess and her 'unfortunate' mood - *all because Iambre would not admit her mistake* – sat on Solancei's shoulder like an invisible gargoyle, gnawing at her temper, so that even the idle chatter between the two messengers to her right (who'd elected to dismount to spare their horses) now thoroughly annoyed her.

Gods, and so did that dog! And Anchan'Chi defend her - *or she'd skin the beast* - that flecking dog had better stop barking soon or she'd lose her composure! She'd have to suffer that fall from South-Point again. *Not gleeful knowledge! However, if it helped make the day specific...*

She chose to forego a sigh - that fall had hurt and it would again but it was only a memory - not real!. And because it was easy, she thought herself into place then; into a point, she knew well; a point that was embarrassing to say the least, and as she did, she drew a deep breath, held it tight in her lungs through the bond with the Veranto.

It made eternity linger on the cusp of awareness, but only for a blink, then she cut loose the last ties to the present...

A sleep-like haze rolled forth. Only, it was not like sleep, for one could not consciously build a dream beforehand – not like that, anyway – but in some ways it mimicked the sensation, she allowed. In this state, however, she felt the very moment where her breath began to slow in the body she was still connected to and she was aware too as her mind began to roll her 'forward' into the past. This time she had longer to observe her own transition and it was not unlike meditation, reminding her of the point in the process when her mind seemed to blur, then unhook from the fabric of her existence...

And yet this still required a level of concentration that made her gasp in effort. *Once... twice...*

Her eyes shot wide open and like earlier, she was no longer in the stuffy firelit cell beneath Castle Zanzier; her limbs were no longer tethered to a macabre bench of torture and her mind was no longer bound by questions or uncertainty. Above her head, the blazing sun stood high in a sky void of clouds, baking down on her back which was instantly as hot as the dark-grey sands along the edges of Lake Etruia, midsummer.

Mercy, and once again she was not alone in her suffering either, for that same sun beat relentlessly against the back of every single man, woman, and animal in Iambre Actarione's substantial retinue. *And Gods, it was hot...*

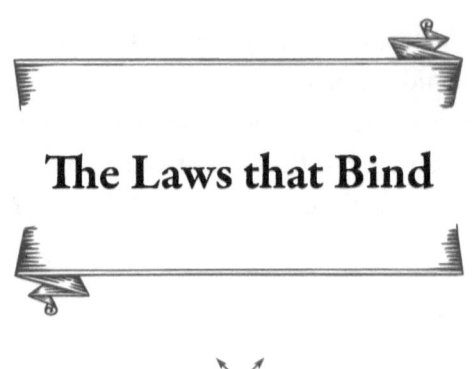

The Laws that Bind

MALANDAR SWALLOWED a choice Venzoian oath. Much as he hated it, that language had always lent itself perfectly to the obscenity of dysfunctional outbursts – however, it would not help his current problem even the tiniest speck now, so the purpose lost credence.

And what to do? It was an intriguingly frustrating question; one he did not need blunt swearing or the fictional speech of dead friends to remind him of, yet he supposed there was merit in his mind's strange machinations. *Odd, but for a Human, Richarmarlan Envalair had never been the forgiving kind. Odd, but his late friend would not have stopped today either, and had Malandar but followed suit, would everything in this hexed existence perhaps have looked a little less uncertain?*

Black and white. That had been Richarmarlan's view of the world. Especially after he became the Guardian. It had meant trouble: Malandar had lost tally of the many occasions. Still, no stranger to 'cause and effect', Marlan Envalair had never been one to shy away from the repercussions if he felt a task must be done. It had made the man and Guardian exceptionally clever at demarcating limits; exceptionally gifted at semantics and evading the precise word of the Maker's Laws. *Clever yes - and when it mattered, perfectly remorseless, too!*

The irony cut: silver beckoning.

Malandar was part-Elvern, true. For someone who knew as much as Marlan, perhaps more, about how to sidle and avoid, about how and when to bend or be cut-throat, he'd admired his friend's ingenuity – perhaps even envied it a little - but at the crux he'd never possessed Marlan's ability to justify everything to suit his own agenda or needs. *Not like that, though the allure...*

But to overstep the line...? *There was 'heritage'. And then there was 'Heritage'.* Malandar could kill without a second thought, and letting go...

Oh but letting go was easy. Too easy even. The black weaves of magic that stained his arms to the elbows and pierced his heart to grow too-alive with every slowed beat, the actual physical proof that reining back was still the salvation!

Yet though it was no longer so, once upon a time, the man he'd been: a bastard known for his quirky humour, blazing magic and occasionally killing sword, would've hesitated not a heartbeat before sending these cowards Beyond - it had been the law of his nature and though it assuredly shouldn't, he recognised it was what called to him now with more power than... than he could remember experiencing in 'forever'.

But the Laws were different for the Upper Circle; for the Guardians – and despoiling the gift of life without proper sanction was, and ever would be, a crime in Alérathnar's eyes! Indeed, breaking faith with the Maker's Laws carried repercussions – and rightly so - but that was not the only true reason why Malandar had never quite wished to embrace Marlan's 'fickle' views post-Guardianship as extensively as his friend might have encouraged.

For Richarmarlan had lead with the heart: with intelligence, but also with little fear of the wider consequences. It had been what so often absolved the other Guardian of true blame, no matter the extent of his trespasses - however by this token, Malandar had rarely dared risk the same - in his case, for the very fear of those wider consequences!

The Maker's Laws had to mean something; they had to remain his conscience throughout: a sort of help to guide his purpose as sworn and directed, for if not...

Yet in the back of his mind, he could 'feel' his former friend laughing softly. *'You know what you must do...'*

Malandar grimaced faintly. Richarmarlan would have thought little of striking down these men, true. He would've struck fast and he would've struck hard: the group had attacked him – it was all the reason needed - but Malandar had abandoned these old principles: a bargain of personal nature with Alérathnar the Maker to finally pacify the inner feral struggle of his split blood and heritage, and it had saved him, but where was the Maker now? It could not be a coincidence that he experienced this level of strain presently; it simply could not.

Clasping at straws, the First Guardian shook himself of the lingering affront.

Knowing that he was arguing with only himself, he was splitting hairs but it seemed prudent: a way to help him recall his oaths – and in the literal sense of the word, one might argue that these three men had actually not attacked, so by default – no matter the urges - he had not the right to ignore his binding words to the Maker. Fine yes, so they'd been part of the group who'd sought him out, but they hadn't followed through; when it came to the crux, they hadn't...

For an infinity, the temptation did not pass as it continued to pull - twisting something best laid dormant within, but Malandar knew the men's abstinence had to count. Without the Marker's direct influence, he feared it doubly important that it must!

He killed an oblique smile.

He was not Guardian Envalair. Not at all. If he had been, many a current thing would be different. Marlan might once have been right in some assumptions, but over two-thirds of Ostravah paid regular homage to every deity they could name in one sentence without triggering conflict, and Malandar could not believe they were all touched by madness. The idea was unfeasible, and so – although his shadow side had still to catch up - he already knew that he wouldn't go raising his weapons - magic or other - in order to send three petrified thieves Beyond.

Tempted to sigh, he refrained, but as sure as the Quickening, it was a relief to also know that the Maker's Laws still held him: that the bargain once made was still binding. And so, for now, rule or ruin, even with what little magic this realm retained, Alérathnar had extended his peace over this situation; rule or ruin, and so Malandar must uphold it to stand firm.

With a notion of aloof approval flowing down his runes, Malandar slowly relaxed Heruvar till the blade hovered just above his knees. In his core, it felt right - but for all his sustained, compelling reasoning, in his heart and mind, there was a yet glimmer of doubt that should have belonged in the past. *Had Richarmarlan not been right? Had he not stated over and over that once touched by the Mad Ones, a person would always be susceptible to the Chaos, should it come visiting again? What if all these God-fearing people of Ostravah were already lost?*

Subtle hints of his former wrath threatening to swirl back into life, for one long, hard moment, he clenched Heruvar's hilt to focus and prevent himself from raising the sword again.

That old compulsion begged. It was like the caress of a shunned, but coveted lover, the idea always tempting; the memory always drawing him. Exactly opposite to what he'd hoped for, the lad on the right had begun mouthing something that sounded like a prayer, and as his lips moved to whisper under each staggered breath, the boy's eyes on Malandar turned glassy - as though willing himself into believing that the First Guardian was but a shade of a vision and thereby not real.

It might have sent the First Guardian back over the edge, but in a flash of near-sentient understanding, Malandar tasted the essence behind the muttered words. *They were as empty as beings the supposedly called upon; without power; without effect - because the lad didn't really believe...*

Ever the last to release its hold of him, the stain of magic on his skin tore at his resolve for one more fleeting moment, but the lad's empty prayers had finally caught Malandar tight. *For now, this had to be over, and he knew a sliver of strange relief: something that didn't belong either.*

Mercy, but the reality was that he could not fight against his nature indefinitely without the Maker – not anymore. Break the Laws; take one step back towards that which his uncle had craved of him to embrace for millennia - and that which Malandar sought to slay, might yet still rise.

To the First Guardian, nothing was worth that: least of all the killing of three 'sheep'. To Richarmarlan it might have been, but for Malandar, that way lay madness - and besides, he would not oblige his uncle either. He hadn't ever before and he did not intend to back down now! This entire situation stank. Stank of something wrong and rotten...

With the sounds of the men's hard breaths, the retching, and the stench already slowly rising from the carnage to stick in the back of the throat, Malandar tried to ignore the buzzing in his head that seemed to tuck at his awareness. Now, without threat to qualify the presence of naked steel, Heruvar had become a deadened lead-weight in his hand: another sure sign the time for killing was over - yet as he'd regained control of himself, something still seemed wrong; something beyond the scope of his personal issues; something...

Malandar looked down at the closest dead robber: the one who'd lost his axe, then an arm, and Heruvar sank a notch further. If one was willing to split hairs, one might possibly argue that the man was still alive. Physically at least, he was still breathing - however, it did not alter the fact that he was bleeding to death, nor that the 'allocated potion' of pain and shock had already rendered him unconscious: a state, from which he was wholly unlikely to recover.

Feeling hollow, waylaid, Malandar looked away with sudden new insights brewing.

He'd almost been too side-blinded to notice, but with the death of the Vessel, Silicia'Cha's 'perfume' no longer clogged the air and he was left here with three petty criminals of minimal concern. Just like the others, they'd probably have been sworn to the Vessel Captain – or at least, to whom the man had been before Silicia'Cha claimed him - but in truth they hardly looked the kind of men who would have questioned which deity their gang pretended to honour if there'd been a promise of gold in the pocket.

Malandar chewed on the observation for a blink, the belated wake-up chime striking an imaginary chord to steel-wrap him in the truth only just realised: a truth that indicated the Vessel might very well have been the only true zealot to begin with, which meant that the rest of the men-

For a heartbeat, another multitude of unusual 'vibes' coiled themselves along his runes whilst the First Guardian registered his own folly.

So he might have managed to stay his sword finally, but it had verily been too late because the thing that hadn't correlated; the little nagging uncertainty that he'd ignored, now seemed blazingly obvious...

Silicia'Cha's influence had lived and died with the Captain of this band, not his men! Yet, in the heat of conflict and contact, and with all his damned inner jinns at work, Malandar had been too caught up to pay proper attention and hence he'd missed the obvious. It meant that no matter which way he turned it, *no matter what his intentions*, he'd assuredly 'taken life' in breach of the Maker's Laws, and so...

The urge to curse returned, now finally draining the last fine filigrees of lingering magic from his skin. *Mercy, though a conceited witch, could Silicia'Cha really have been that clever? Had she planned this? Or had She simply gotten lucky?*

As it balanced - *black hex on the vixen and all her kind!* - it almost didn't matter, for whatever 'the design' - *whether a deliberate trap or plain ugly luck* - this was a mistake that would eventually cost him all the same!

Though the Vessel was still dead and Silicia'Cha could not physically touch him, it suddenly felt to Malandar like She had just reached out across the Void to slap him full in the face. Of course, there was every chance that She had not purposely planned this development – nevertheless, She must have known he'd react to mete out punishment as First Guardian in the form of self-defence and righteous protection. He'd caught scent of Her stench clinging to the group and that had been the trigger, but Her control over the men had been a ruse; she had cloaked them with Her essence through the Vessel: a trick to think them all sworn to the Elated. *Her presence; her madness... it had been an illusion, but black fell had he just 'danced to oblige' just the same!*

Derision biting, Malandar was aware that this would not have happened had the magic flows still been right! Indeed, had magic still run true, he would have read the signs: could have killed the Vessel whilst incapacitating the re-mainder of the unfortunate gang with a few simple Weaves – yet blinded by the sudden attack, he'd substituted common sense for rash action, never pausing to notice if any of the renegades had 'felt' true or not.

Similarly, aware that the Goddess had Her standards, magic or no, he might have paused for long enough to notice a second part of the truth too; might have paused to recall that this rat-tack collection of clothes and armour could not have belonged to any of Silicia'Cha's actual ilk. *Homespun tunics and patched-up breeches, leather chaffs, poorly mended hauberks or missing-link chain shirts did not belong. She would've demanded better of Her zealots. She always did – to set Her apart from Endar'Cha's scum!*

Not quite knowing how to interpret this mistake, Malandar had to admit that the deity had been more cunning than usual. In place of true affiliation, She'd settled for an alliance of a temporary convenience – possibly in exchange for the promise of 'easy' plunder, and why not? She'd needed eyes on the ground: the Captain himself had obviously been willing to sell Her this plea-sure for a fee – and, true to form, Silicia'Cha had made easy promises that She was bound by no seal of honour or law to uphold.

Weariness gnawing at his spirit for his oversight, the First Guardian needn't look to the dead as a reminder of how they now wore the varying marks of their quick demise like awards of bravery and commendation that She would never give them: like royal sashes of magenta splendour and service medals of crimson honour that could never be rescinded. It made Silicia'Cha the only winner. These men hadn't expected Her self-serving menace and transcending insincerity to stretch quite so far, and as for himself...

Yes, the vixen had gotten Her answer here today; had played him to Her advantage, knowing full well that whether She set Her dogs on a random traveller or not, She'd have lost nothing to have Her suspicions investigated. And on a quiet road... an unexpected attack...

A lone traveller would've stood little chance against nine armed men; would probably not have been found before winter either, whereas a Guardian, of course...

A small movement caught his eye. *The three survivors again. It was disquieting. The praying one was sliding to his knees, lips never stilling...*

Malandar quivered and shifted his stance, vaguely wondering how to get these men on their way with the least amount of bother now, but for a few blinks longer, his thoughts remained occupied with the Mad Ones.

If Silicia'Cha had thought to be scouting for the return of the Upper Circle already, the others would be recruiting their spies too.

Forcing his hand, causing him trouble with the Maker's Laws might or might not have been Her intentions, but when all was dusted and weighed, he was left with just a few simple questions: questions as to what the fickle creature would choose to do with the knowledge of the Guardians' return? *Act or wait? Share or taunt?*

Malandar resisted the urge to close his eyes and re-centre his spirit like he'd resisted everything else. He thought he knew the answers too readily - and this cleared his mind like an Oridaboard swept clean of pieces for a new round. *Henceforth, he'd have to have a care. He did not want to leave a trail for them to follow; he could perhaps be forgiven to react like a star-crossed half-wit once, but to do so twice?!*

At the moment, Human spies could find the Twins just as well as he – probably faster too – and he mustn't let it come to that. Whether She'd tricked him or not, Silicia'Cha had obviously seen him deliberately refrain from using his most powerful weapon – magic - and though She must be aware of the state that gripped the realms, She'd still be wondering why he'd chosen to lead with the sword!

Infinitely relieved that the Mad Ones did not share with the Guardians the benefit of the Sight, Malandar nevertheless knew the danger of them discovering his and the others' current weakness. *There were any and many ways to find out, and if they did-*

A small tendril of weariness shifted within him and he narrowed his gaze with displeasure that wasn't all linked to his Guardian instinct. *Whether he could justify using the Neidar Ba'raie or not, the deity had just forced his hand, that much was clear - and he did not like being 'manoeuvred'. Black hex, he did not!*

Still, seemed like he could never quite escape that particular curse though: seemed like people had wanted him to yield to their needs for as long as he could recall and to this day it still suited his spirit poorly! That Silicia'Cha moved to use him too - even subtly - was not a surprise, considering that manipulation was one of Her most 'endearing' qualities, but She was too bold now and all that needed doing to top Her list with a cap of perfection was for him to complete the renegades' sentencing without mercy.

And it could have been perfect, he reflected: him eradicating all traces of Her 'discovery' so that she alone possessed the knowledge of his presence. Yes, that would surely have suited Her – and if those men had not lost their nerve and raised a thought for caution, it would've been a done deed.

To Malandar it was a situation laced with irony. Silicia'Cha had snapped at his heels today, but by Her doings, the ancient hag had unwittingly committed an error. *And so his hand was moved for him. Simple. He must go get the Neidar Ba'raie...*

His choice brought forth a sense of peace and a sliver of his old serenity, assuring him that oddly he could not be too far out of line. However, if he must indeed attempt to tamper with 'the ill-advised'; if he were to create a 'link' and slap a 'seal' on it in order to steal a little leverage, he'd have to do so before securing the Tarvia. Otherwise, he'd risk not only the Twins but also the hazard of having to deal with a fey well of power want to act as it pleased whilst having to dodge yet more opportunistic attacks like this one. *First Guardian or not – Malandar did not relish this kind of struggle right up until the Veils began to draw apart. As demonstrated today, it was just too uneconomic!*

The Guardian exhaled one long breath and felt a sliver of unknown emotion penetrate and further shatter his normally simmering detachment. *The lingering sight of death and waste; of his own lacking control... Silicia'Cha's error or not: he was the First of the Upper Circle! This would never have happened if the magic had not been torn! Never.*

Still, because it seemed it must, his attention reluctantly wandered back to the survivors. Though he could not act on it, an uneasy part of him twitched just one final time. The three wretches had chosen the conflict; delayed his progress – in a certain light their offence merited capital punishment - but black hex on the bitch, he was not going to play this game in the direction She'd stirred. If She wanted rid; if She wanted no traces of Her discovery, then She'd have to do better next time and not hang Her demands on him – for now, there'd been enough killing!

Resolutely, Malandar shifted his balance.

Relaxing his stance to release the remaining tension from the situation, he abruptly spun Heruvar up and around, the action a curt expert whirl – only to ram the blade back into its black-lacquered sheath with precise unerring fluency.

It seemed right to have serenity back once more, and he wondered if these men carried any perception of the various shades of 'luck' afforded them here today? Verily the Realm of Ostravah had been Marlan's charge: rightly it should've been Marlan in his place here now. And in his place, Malandar felt sure the other Guardian would've written their Ending into the Tapestry! *Would any of the men ever be able to comprehend what exactly had happened here? Could they?*

By the look on their faces, Malandar thought he might accurately predict the answer to this question as well. The sheathing of his sword had failed to impress upon them his leniency; they still carried themselves like gallows-bound and in a flash, new discontent riled his spirit.

He just wanted the men gone from sight and senses – and soon would not be fast enough! Their fear wafted in the air like a perfume gone bad – *an unpleasant reminder of Silicia'Cha's influence* - and Malandar deliberately looked away then, hoping his lack of attention might just be the thing to sway their minds to beat it for safety. With dull incidental interest, he noted the man with the missing arm no longer guilty of breathing; the one he'd run through still appeared to be fluctuating in and out of consciousness, his 'will' so obviously still fighting the fleeting function of his body in a useless conflict that would have only one outcome. *It was stupidly clumsy: he should have aimed for the heart!*

Malandar clenched his jaw and shook in his head minutely. *Yes, he should have aimed for the heart, just as he should have realised the truth behind this attack, just as he should've used steel to kill the Vessel and magic to incapacitate the rest but instead he'd done everything backwards: had committed a mistake and thereby an improbable situation fraught by fatality!* With what he now realised about the situation, he should have healed the injured too. Verily, for any men not proven true-sworn to Chaos, Malandar had an obligation to set right what wrongs he'd caused – but for once he just couldn't find the will to oblige the Maker.

What little magic he still had left, they did not deserve; it was not spite, nor malice, only fact, and besides – the 'ghost' of Guardian Envalair was right: to heal them Malandar would have to lay a hand on them. In their moment of recovery and lingering confusion the Goddess could find them in a heartbeat and though they may not have felt inclined to embrace her influence earlier – once hale and suddenly face to face with the man who'd just cut them, many would grasp at strands to get payback. *Price... everything for a price...*

"Please, good Sir... mercy? Mercy, M'lord, mercy..."

The quiet whimper projected penitence, but the sentiment cut deeper as the words ripened with terror like spoiling pickle berries left unharvested to go to seed.

Malandar adjusted his focus back to the men but he could not identify the speaker. Blunt resignation filled him. *Why were they even still there? Even sheep would have run by now!*

"By the spirits, would you just go!" he hissed with an abrupt gesture of dismissal and watched them all jump with fright although his action had not been threatening. It gave them leeway and pause though - as if time itself seemed to hold its breath - and for a blink, no one moved as their eyes searched him for falsehood.

To Malandar it felt like an eternity, but he did nothing to contradict the intended dismissal and with nothing more than a sudden twitch, the lad who'd been on his knees seemed to gain a measure of hope, for as he looked directly at the First Guardian, the fear seemed to waver for long enough to render him capable of recalling that he still had legs.

Unsteady as a new-born fawn, the lad clambered to his feet, each tiny move accompanied by a stutter of caution as though to test the strength of both his own muscle and Malandar's goodwill.

Embracing new serenity, the First Guardian looked away once more. Through the corner of his eye, he was aware as the youth retreated one careful step, then another. At the same time, he could feel the oldest man stare at his young comrade with something akin to surprise and awe, something that seemed to register like a deep heavy vibe of disbelief in the air.

Malandar levelled his eyes on the sky-line, deliberately dismissing the men from mind, whilst forcing himself to consider other issues. He figured it'd be just a measure short of five days before he reached the walls of Zanzier Town, perhaps longer if the terrain was still as coarse as he recalled it, and the horses gave out. But Zanzier Town was the marker. Alérathnar willing, the Tarvia would not be much farther, he sensed - providing he'd actually gotten his bearings right in this turned-around world, of course! Atop of that, however, he'd better take into the equation his newly justified need of a detour to secure the Neidar Ba'raie, too – an exercise which might add an extra couple of days to the overall journey if it all went well, and if it did not-

With the approach of night proper and another day gone, his ailing sense of patience suddenly flared.

"Black fell! Shagetz dah, khristaranur!" he exclaimed, suddenly vexed to the hilts of his swords.

Aware that the obscenity of harsh foreign words would do nothing to aid the situation – and somehow not caring - he tilted his chin to bring his gaze abruptly back on the men. It matched the new-flash stab of nuisance that assailed him, but he still didn't care as he sent them a cutting glance.

"The Veils be cursed! Enough! What don't you people understand?! I have given you grace – now would you just go! Go!"

The sheer tone of his command ought to have been enough to cut through the three men's reserve, but perhaps they were not only idiots but also halfwits - and with a fiery glint in his eyes now for their inability to simply comply, Malandar gave in and drew upon a sliver of the coveted magic from his Call Rune.

The contact was like a balm against his mind as he connected latent Power with personal Will and wove Intent - and too late then to regret the waste, he reached out into their thoughts without refinement.

"You will all go now or - help me Alérathnar! - I *will* change my mind," he grated at them with cold promise and released the spell.

"You will forget about me and what you saw! Don't ever look back! Don't ever come back! Recall if you would, that the being you know as the deity Silicia'Cha can have no hold over you; to think Her capable of influencing anything but Her own ego is downright delusional and She is a menace to be denied! Remember this and never again be fooled by Her or other deities' promises of protection or riches! Now go spread this Truth and praise Alérathnar for the gift of your lives!"

And with that, he repelled them: a brute mental shove to shift their focus. It saw the flat-nosed youth and 'prayer-boy' stumble into witless action, just a blink before the last man dropped his weapons as if burned by their touch.

They bolted like deer then; mindless. With little attention to their chosen path or the trailing Heinar.

Malandar blinked as he watched them go. By some miracle, they managed to move faster than he would have thought possible over this ground as they scampered. He regretted the loss of warmth he'd relinquished as he'd released the Weave, but he guessed that was only normal. *Not one man looked back.* In a while, they'd be remembering little other than the fear associated with something intangible experienced on this day, and of course the message that *the Mad Ones* could not be trusted. *If it didn't quite pay his dues, it was a start...*

A random gust of wind swept his hair and the panels of his long coat into a shallow dance and Malandar's attention was diverted by a perplexing shiver of cold down his spine.

Curious... this was new - a Spell-Weaver was never cold: something to do with their Affinity and ability to persuade the flows and the way in which these eventually became part of said Weaver, because each would practise until the magic was as integral to their life as the ability to breathe.

Malandar could not recall when he'd last been cold - if ever. *The Power was warmth...*

Rather than linger on the puzzle - *at the moment there were too many to count* - he set the thought aside, and watched the men's rushed retreat as they scrambled without concern for life or limbs. At one point the yellow-haired youth tumbled forward on the uneven ground to fall head over heels, legs flopping wildly, but he laboured to gather himself up off the wiry undergrowth to continue his flat-out run and cover lost ground.

Then they were gone through a gap in the far-off bushes. Peace seemed a breathing thing...

Malandar stared blindly at the spot for a few heartbeats longer, his mind as quiet as sleep finally. Their horses must be near, he imagined, though not so close as to have given them away in the first place and as the memory of the gang's relative near-success played over inside his mind, he knew a blink of displacement. As it had been meant to do, his Spirit Rune had shifted the chill finger of healing towards the place on his neck where the foreign metal had demanded blood earlier - there'd been nothing unusual about that – however, the breeze of the uneven edge of iron against his pulse had been something else entirely!

It was still utterly alive: he could feel the mixed metal of the blade ride into contact, could still feel the way the shallow cut had lacerated the upper layers of his skin with enough severity to turn the wound momentarily icy whilst the magic pooled to restore his skin beyond flaw; and he could still feel his own surprise...

However brief the injury, the mere fact that it'd happened had undeniably touched him deeper than the subsequent physical cut - as had the near-utter failure of his Battle Rune to warn him of the danger before they'd been crawling all over him! *And the Maker defend: it was unheard of!* There was a wispy, two-inch tear in the fabric across the right shoulder of his coat - a thing he hadn't noted till now - and though the cut had not landed hard enough to touch skin, the mere fact that he'd not avoided this either, made him all too aware of his own rusty skills with the blades he carried.

But Guardians did not get rusty! He did not get rusty! By the Tower of Ishla'rus! He did not!

Frustratingly, Malandar had no glorious answer to explain what had happened in those few moments but it was disturbing how close that Vessel had managed to get without his senses springing any kind of alarm, not Venzoian-related. Sure, the slip-up with the sword had been small, but what of the next time?

It was almost inconceivable, but 'next time' it might not be as easy to shake it off as an 'unfortunate event'. Next time he might have the Tarvia with him – perhaps even the Alscara - and then it might well be a shadow-crawler creeping up on him – or a whole contingent...

'So go get the Sentient Magic,' his mind seemed to chant with a hint of a dead friend's voice, 'just go get it, and next time don't stop till they're all dead. Next time, do better...'

To Create a Moment Out of Time

I am dreaming, Solancei thought, semi-conscious of the fact that she was sinking deeper into her own memories, yet also strangely uninvolved now, as her mind steered her to the purpose almost randomly whilst she was just the sleepwalker not in control of their own actions.

From another world, she felt a faint disturbance then. *Was it fear? Anger?*

Her attention slid away. Her breath was so shallow now, the idea of such emotion so removed from her thoughts, that she paid the sound of the distant roar no mind. This world was where she needed to be now and the illusion she'd called was rapidly turning so tactile that she deliberately let go just a little more so that she could look around her.

Everything seems so real, she thought, the marvel of it slow to penetrate too. *But this was everything mundane and forgotten, achingly detailed and bathed in clarity – as though she was there again. In the past... not a dream now, but the present.*

And indeed... *as if on cue, dirt crunches softly between her molars as she pensively nibbles the inside of her cheek. It makes her swallow in disgust. She recalls that emotion now. It's just how she feels, or felt, or is feeling... and the mild hum of lingering pain across her lower abdomen is likewise the same! Women's trouble... she hates this time of month; Riselta's concoctions do not seem to have the desired effect these days - but this is good, a part of her whispers: go deeper, this is just what you are searching for...*

For a blink, her head spins. The air is humid – hot and slightly gritty with the fine particles of dust that is produced by the mass of hooves and wheels and feet. It lingers in the air, dirtying those unlucky to come behind the vanguard. She recalls that the already-reluctant breeze has died sometime during the last hour or so; laments now, how nothing relieves the heat.

She remembers she was uncomfortable – and realises that because of the memory, *she is uncomfortable!* Her eyes sting from fatigue yet again; from lack of sleep because the nights here are too stuffy and she spends too much time awake wondering how to approach Klaas with the *'Veranto thing'.*

She also remembers that in spite of her veil, she squints a lot too. Because the sun seems to reflect in every small buckle or shiny surface within a league - *wish that I had a hat, like Ina: a new headache threatens.* But she is here now. Just as she needs to be and she thinks she remembers why this is important...

She sighs but the veil barely shudders, it's that tight. They've been travelling north for days now, a small mercy she is thankful for, since going south would've put the sun directly in her eyes, but the pace gripes her. *It is not really any kind of pace is it? And she's taken to calling it 'a waddle' whenever she can push Iambre's stubborn face in it.* But Iambre does not rise to her words for this pace suits the Princess very well, and that's the truth of it! *This is what she'd wanted all along: delays and more delay. Shame Iambre has failed to factor in much more than her own interest; shame she'd not been able to predict what a total karat nuisance this detour was want to become for everyone else who actually has a job to perform whilst on this journey.*

Another sigh escapes her. The compressed, hard ground is rocky and un-even – *treacherous* - with hidden rabbit holes or irregularities where the ground has somehow collapsed down behind tufts of vegetation so that a horse will break its leg if not careful. *Has anyone else ever traversed this land? It seems unlikely for this is the Wilderness,* she thinks dully, unimpressed. In fact, she ought to jump off South-Point and walk - she'll be devastated if the animal is injured because of her inattention - but the gelding is clever and seems to have developed a knack for feeling out his own way, so she stays put and lets the horse pick the path he wishes.

Gods, but when will it end? She crinkles her nose as dust wheedles in despite the tightly-wound scarf that hides her face. This terrain, supposedly, covers an area bigger than the south-western corner of Etruia but that concludes all common features. Not only is this land undomesticated, it is also a good many vengeful degrees warmer, as well as drier by a margin of... *oh, at least a hundred barren rivers!*

Furthermore, it is seemingly endlessly flat, but for the dry scrubs and spo-radic clusters of trees and desiccated gardens of self-seeded Heinar. *Fleck, and I once thought Etruia was hot... well not so now.*

Blinking rapidly to clear her watering eyes, Solancei focuses her gaze on the horizon of the arid landscape. The narrow slit in her black and silver veil that leaves just her eyes uncovered seems almost a hindrance rather than a benefit: the light is too sharp; she should have worn a full veil rather than this, but that's even more unbearable in this heat.

She feels the line of her mouth tighten without fail, but at least she is not alone in favouring this attire: the soldiers, the waggoneers, and the coach-men alike – they all wear scarves or folded triangles of cloth in a similar fashion. It protects against sun and dust sure, but it still makes her feel like a Shaz renegade – or an assassin – but maybe that's just her?

She blinks again but her eyes are itchy and her head is heavy. She tries to stay alert, but there is nothing or no one to entertain her interest: the mes-sengers behind her natter like washerwomen – thankfully not about how un-reasonable Iambre has become, but rather about someone's engagement back home to a woman without appeal - and then, about the exciting prospects that the King might manage to acquire a staggering ten Afhpar pure-bloods as soon as the secret trade routes are engaged. *It's monotony made real and as she has done of late, she lets her mind go numb.* It sends her senses fuzzy, almost as if she cannot function in this heat, but it delays the headaches, so she has begun to consider the exchange favourable.

Solancei blinks again, momentarily assailed by the oddest idea then that she's forgotten something... *something important...* but a jolt – a stumbling lurch, really - chases the thought from her mind as she is forced to steady herself in the saddle just in time before another step sends her horse into a hidden dip that tilts her sharply forward. She worries for a blink, but South-Point only snorts as his next step takes them back up onto higher ground.

The pitch and the rocking movement makes her sway and for a moment she is assailed by confusion: her mind feels clouded like on a day where she has overslept and Klaas barges into her chamber, issuing scolding commands in such an unending stream of words and information that she misses half the in-structions whilst trying to wake up.

She cannot explain why but it feels like she's missed half of the instructions now too; as though something needs repeating, but she is bloody astride South-Point, not leaping from her bed like an upset crow from a tree. *Perhaps she is just tired?* Being at odds with her best friend is exhausting but what can she do? *She tells me I am stubborn, but I am not, am I?*

She shakes her head. With the way her horse is adjusting to the ground with every step, with all this lurching and rocking, she feels ready to drop asleep in the saddle and the idea horrifies her enough to sit up and force the impending yawn down. *Sleep in the saddle? No, you cannot sink that low! That would be beastly!*

Somewhere ahead she hears the loud call to halt and looks up in surprise. Bleary-eyed, yet with that lingering edge of urgency still riding her, she realises then with a pang that the entire caravan is slowly grinding to a standstill. It is not a scheduled stop for it is barely noon, and yet it is meant to happen, but how does she know this? For the realm, she can't quite seem to recall something important; perhaps something to do with Iambre's schedule or something to do with her own training assignments? *And why are we stopping now?* She thinks she already knows why, but can't seem to recall this either: the heat is cooking her brain under this veil!

Solancei halts South-Point and shifts his green leather reins into her left hand so that she can hunch forward to cross her forearms and relax against the saddle's crescent-shaped pommel. It alleviates those damnable stomach pains and is a comfortable perch too, for though the pommel is not as tall as that of a jousting saddle, the green cloth and black leather padding offers support and - though she is not keen to admit it - a chance to rest. The impromptu stop is the only thing that's happened for hours and it offers a break in the tedium, so she pays a little more attention than usual as she watches the procedures unfold.

People are rapidly approaching from all around: two squires, the head of logistics, the statutory dozen guards that surround the royal carriage, the ever-present trio of messengers and their runners...

Then Iambre's head pokes through the carriage window to invoke attention in an instant, but Solancei turns her eyes away. Iambre's headpiece of three linked golden bands seems to glitter like flashing fascinators in the places where they are part-visible through the weaves of her hair and the effect cuts into Solancei's vision like tiny sharp barbs.

The incidental thought that they'll be days still before they finally reach their destination, passes through her mind and catches her attention and she recalls yet again that they will be late. *But how is it possible that she should know such a thing? Perhaps the days are simply blending into one now? For sure, the heat is certainly making her dozy...*

The cloth itching, she rubs the bridge of her nose between the thumb and forefinger, exhaling. It takes in-ordinary long for her to bring her faculties to heal and this odd disorientated state of mind seems to linger along with that stupidly nagging idea that she *really* needs to focus on something important! *On her...? On her purpose here, perhaps? Is that it?*

New uncertainty leaves her queasy. *Purpose? What purpose?* Somehow she can't lock the thought down for long enough to bring true recall. Instead, she remembers trivia. She remembers that several horses have thrown shoes or gone lame or both; she remembers that Lieutenant del'Draventar, Bilandro Metavo's Second-in-Command, has had to loan the King's black Rayon – a supposed present for Lord Tan'Xaviar – and that the costly stallion is about to stumble and lose a shoe too. She remembers also, that there'll be no bath for another three days still, not even for Iambre. The water is just too scarce and has been rationed for drinking and cooking - and with an ill flicker against her peace of mind, she has to wonder how she can be so sure?

She lets out a sigh; tries to let it go, but the idea of something forgotten – or unfinished - leaves her irritated; slightly frustrated, and definitely worried. *Not a good combination for her...*

Somewhere a dog is barking again. Solancei blinks and without warning, a notion of indisputable déjà-vu descends; then something flares in her core, almost in response it seems, and all at once she feels both hot and cold. *There is something about that dog...*

She shakes her head again. *Perhaps she's about to suffer heatstroke? Perhaps she ought to get off this horse before she falls off?*

Falls off... yes, that too seems to awaken something familiar; something she cannot quite reach...

Solancei inhales deeply, rolls her neck and absent-mindedly reaches to rub her throat through the veil. The skin feels sore to the touch she realises in that usual resigned manner of hers, which means she barely cares though she briefly wonders when she's managed to do herself *this* injury?

There is no déjà-vu attached to that one, however; no sixth sense, and she lets it go. The quiet commotion is still stirring around Iambre's vehicle...

She glances around casually. Familiar faces surround her, and from the people that are near enough that she can spy their emotions and hear their words, it seems that everyone is as fed up as she. *But it's no wonder.* They've been on the roads for so long now, that she's all but forgotten what it feels like to sleep in her own bed back in Servangar; so long, she's almost forgotten what it feels like to have the luxury of privacy.

A crooked smile breaks her lips apart underneath the veil. *It has been a long journey, but at least she has Iambre!* Some of these men and women are not that lucky. Some of these people have had to leave loved ones and family behind in the name of duty, and they long to go home now. They are nearly at the end of this journey and she can hear them in the night: *with the end so nearly in sight, why does Iambre deliberately delay?*

Embarrassment seeps in. Solancei knows the answer - *as does Bilandro Metavo,* she suspects - but the truth is hers to keep a secret, even if no one is pleased about this impromptu 'detour' across the Wilderness. *'Of all the places to go-',* she hears them whisper, *'-it makes little sense. Has the Princess lost her mind? Is she taken with an illness of the mind'?*

Solancei's smile turns wry, then sour. Only a few concerned 'spirits' have approached Solancei directly with their questions or worries - maybe for fear of what reply she might give, maybe for fear that her answer will be 'wrapped in blades' as usual, but she has heard them ask others. Speculations are never kind. *Iambre come to your senses soon, I beg you! You cannot delay the enviable, my friend, only alienate the people who love you.*

Interred thus in her own thoughts, Solancei does not instantly pay much attention as the excited sounds of dogs creep nearer – that is, at least not until one of the company's stout grey mastiffs suddenly tears forward out of nowhere to fly straight under South-Point girth, so fast that the creature's golden-touched coat is but a dust-enveloped blur.

It startles South-Point and the gelding reacts without pause: throws his head up and swerves side-ways with a lurch and a small buck that makes her bounce and scramble to reassemble her faculties. *Then comes the other dog...*

It is all she has time to look up and see the 'supposed danger' as it runs in a straight line towards her. It has no sense nor sight it seems, for it does not stop;

it is almost upon them and her horse is already spooked. She has him in hand though he dances on edge, but the stupid dog is about to trap himself between South-Point's chopping front hooves and she cannot stop it...

Ears flat back, her horse rises up high on his hind legs, coming down nearly vertical as he issues a deep whinnying challenge... the dog swerves with a yelp... *her balance slips...*

In a blink she realises how stupid this is: South-Point has reared with her before, but she has not been unseated in years and yet in that very heartbeat, she just knows - *is deadly sure in fact* - that her backside will hit that dirt below with enough force to pummel the breath from her lungs. There will be no broken bones, no - but her bruises will be spectacular; in fact, she still carries one across her right hip – and the medic will not allow her to ride then - not until they reach the outskirts of Zanzier town. Riselta's 'just in case' will annoy Solancei though, for instead she'll be on a pallet on the floor of the smith's spare wagon, under a green awning amongst the tools and supplies of his trade. *It will be by choice, though. It will be preferable to Iambre's coach, yet less comfortable than South-Point because of the terrain...*

Time seems to slow; she is slipping and she braces herself for the brief free-fall and subsequent bump; ahead the dogs crush into a decent size thicket of near-dead shrubs...*she doesn't know why she closes her eyes... then...*

Nothing!

South-Point's hoofs hit the ground squarely with a heavy 'thud' that makes her lurch forward. *His sides are working like bellows puffing the breath in and out of his nostrils as if he's been run hard... but she has not fallen!*

Strange flat horror grips her. *Not fallen...*

She is acutely aware suddenly, that people are staring at her - some in open-mouthed horror of the disaster that nearly was - some with looks of shocked surprise. *Then time seems to re-set just about in line with her registering the angry shouts of 'heel' and 'to me Rufus' coming from behind.*

Strangely stiff, she turns in the saddle to see the unfortunate handler and his boys come rushing forward in pursuit of their wayward dogs. She is not sure if any of them have seen what just happened but she is too shocked herself to even bring it to his attention - and so, armed with reins and whips, the handler and his group forces on past her, unchallenged.

A few people turn their faces away then, the spectacle done and disaster averted – *a few lose dogs is not enough to give anyone further concern* - but many still just look at her, now with another kind of surprise. Evidently they know her well and must have expected her to give the handler a piece of her mind for his sloppiness - after all, being at fault for the Princess' favourite handmaiden nearly taking a dive in the dirt, is not something anyone would wish himself guilty off: there'd be an ear lashing, perhaps worse...

Or at least there usually would be - and therein lies the surprise. It will probably make for an even more interesting chatter around the camp, than had she actually fallen - and in a flash, she recalls that before – *when she did fall* - she'd been too winded to actually berate the handler, so of course they'd all whispered about that too. *But that was different...*

Confused how her mind seems to continuously 'remember', an icy chill steals over her and she pats a now quiet South-Point on the neck. In truth, it is mostly to steady herself, not the horse, and it occurs to her then that her heart rate has barely altered even when she thought herself about to fall. It is an acknowledgement that makes her strangely light-headed with fear, for something is not right; in fact, something is very much amiss, and she can ignore the lingering few stares easily for she is now too pre-occupied.

To stop her own dread, she turns her attention back towards the royal carriage. There is a total of fifteen people standing in a semi-circle around the left side of the vehicle now and as one man gestures – *she thinks it Sir Mortrat from the wide stocky build and the gleaming silver of the officer's badge that decorate his shoulder* – another man, this one also of the household guard, steps closer so to join the conversation with a few enthusiastic nods.

Iambre, still only head and shoulders visible through the window, nods back and says something that makes Sir Mortrat laugh. It's a familiar scene but Solancei does not feel inspired to join. *You were lucky that you kept your seat... lucky... or else the gossip would've been worse! Except this is not right, because you should have fallen. You knew it would happen - and yet it did not! How did you know this? What is this? What are you missing?*

Suddenly, the imaginary layer of dust that seems to be coating the inside of her throat makes it hard for her to breathe. Part of her feels like she is missing out on something momentous. Right here. Right now. As if her near-fall should have prompted her to do something.

But what?
What indeed?

Stalked by Waiting

SOLANCEI SHIVERS THEN - *in spite of the heat* - she shivers, as the pressure of urgency rekindles. Up ahead, the scenery looks to waver in the mounting heat and her mind does not seem capable of focusing. Somehow the loose dogs have been caught – *good!* And they are whining as they are dragged away to the sound of their master scolding – *again: good!* But as with everything else, her interest seems incidental. Instead, there is something that warns her that 'a time wasting nightmare' is about to unfold around Iambre's carriage, where after it won't be long before the call to camp is made.

The thought sends another cold rush down her spine as a semblance of understanding hits her with a dead certainty she would've given anything to deny. *Because she knows the order of this: knows which way this will happen - and it makes no sense that she should know!* However, as she spies the head groom, now making his way forward towards the gathering – *afoot, so as to spare his precious steeds* - she knows she's right. He will be determined, she recalls, to argue with Captain Metavo that the horses will need a full day and night rest before they can continue, for this ground is too-fickle to sustain their current pace without further incidents, and since they cannot go much slower...

The man's words will inspire pause, then caution. She's watched it all from the ground last time, of course, before the medic completed her examination and forced some bandaging on her. Then Solancei had been brought to the centre of a somewhat escalating discussion just as Iambre was siding with the head groom. Iambre had then taken the advice of the medic, slightly wide-eyed in concern and sheepish with regret that she hadn't realised Solancei had been hurt. *Adding salt to the wound, the medic would insist that Solancei had to be giv-*

en at least a full day's rest, preferably more – and that had been that. Quite literally! Upon Iambre's order, they'd be going nowhere for a good two days, maybe three, and if it had annoyed the 'opposition', they could just not argue with the medic, so camp had been made.

Metavo, of course, had not been pleased with the delay. Not one bit! But perhaps he had not been as bothered about the stop, as he had been about the manner in which Iambre had told him that it was not his decision to make!

Solancei recalled seeing Metavo's already dispassionate face growing virtually blank more times than she could count as of recently, but he clearly refused to give Iambre the pleasure of knowing just how much she irked him, and like any other meeting that had ended in argument, Metavo had simply performed his usual bow void of flourish, then taken his leave. It was all very proper, of course, but it was this exact display of personal restraint that had become yet just another thing that Iambre was not pleased about when it came to Metavo. *But who could blame the man? Iambre... well, she'd made her choice!*

'How can you expect someone to stay around when you have also made it abundantly clear that you do not wish to see their face in any other capacity than that dictated by duty?' Solancei would ask the Princess sweetly this evening. *'How? Indeed, why?'*

But this is all yet to come, it seems, though she is assailed by a bewildering feeling of knowledge and doubt. She absently wonders if her 'not falling' will somehow have made any changes to the order or outcome of the event about to unfold but this thought is even more unsettling than the idea of urgency and she does not pursue it. The groom has reached the carriage now, and Bilan Metavo is making his way closer, as she watches, carefully picking his route so that his roan will not stumble. She wonders – now, as then - if he is perhaps deliberately slow just to spite the difficult Heiress?

"Hot, dusty, dull, monotonous days,-" Metavo had predicted when Iambre *had decided to make these sudden changes to their programme, "-it will not be easy goings in the Wilderness, whereas the river route will! Milady, the river is a natural highway between here and Zanzier! We can even time it with the tides to arrive in the city prior to schedule if you so wish. My Princess... please heed this: do not make us trail across the Wilderness. It is virtually unchartered territory: I guarantee it will cost us!"*

But Iambre, of course, had not given up; she'd set out to annoy Bilan and not a thing could change that, but this had indeed cost them all. Bilan had been right. And it had cost Iambre particularly, for she was increasingly rude towards everyone. Solancei has admitted to herself several times that she ought to intercept the disaster, except...

Except, she doesn't know how to do so.

Iambre and Ina are also emerging from the box they call 'transport' now, stretching their limbs and shielding their eyes as they do, but she knows that Iambre would rather stare straight at the sun these days, than look at the Captain, and thus she will barely acknowledge him today, though his status warrants her respect. The obvious way in which she avoids him will make for dangerous speculations if she does not let up soon. *Iambre please see sense. Please...*

But sooner or later this is bound to come to a head and it cuts Solancei to the heart that she will not be there to stop it! *Cuts... cuts that... that what?*

Feeling confused, she shakes her head.

The moment drags; for a blink, time seems to stop. Somewhere close by, one of those native crow-like birds squawk – *she is used to them now: those large black 'things' that perch on the ground, yet sit as tall as the length of her entire arm* - and she remembers this sound too: like an echo of a dream, just as new feeling of lightheaded nausea envelops her.

For a wonder she manages to dismount, mainly because she knows then that she'll fall if she does not, but as her feet hit the uneven ground, the new migraine sends a spike through her head out of nowhere.

Like some unfit prissy fool overcome by fatigue, her final thought, before the world goes awry, is of Klaas and of how she really must speak to her mentor now. *For you cannot let your condition worsen beyond this and not tell Klaas. You must tell Klaas. You must warn her!*

'But she is not here,' a small voice whispers in her ear, unexpectedly, and her world spins so badly then, that she feels herself shaking with the need to be sick, only she can't. And the voice pecks at her: like the beak of one of those big black crow-like birds dipping and tearing into the still-warm carcass of the horse they'd had to destroy on their first day of 'foray' into the Wilderness. *The first mount to break a cannon bone...*

'No, Klaas is not here! The voice pecks. *You already know this! Klaas is with Tracker Bowmar and that tall, Kheltian Horse-Guard Fe-Fa-something-she-couldn't-remember-the-name.'*

What she does remember, though, is that Klaas is not going to be back in camp until tomorrow.

But you cannot wait that long! Remember?! Iambre is in danger!'

Heart lurching, Solancei looks up towards the carriage, the urgency instilled in her from childhood that she must protect Iambre, instantly flaring - but her head is still spinning and the sharp change makes her vision darken as if all her blood has suddenly run to her head.

Then she is falling, folding really, as though she has no bones to hold her upright - her hold on the saddle suspending - *and still...* there is a heartbeat then, a blink in time, where her mind is suddenly clear. It's not much, but-

'Fashion the Moment Out of Time!' the voice urges, no longer pecking *'Do it soon now, or else you will fail!'*

And that is it! In a blazing flash of insight, the purpose slams back into form and she sees the danger then, the danger which is attached to this kind of exercise. It is elusive: as wispy as a true dream, and as encapsulating as a prison. *Without expert discipline... without... without control...*

Without control, in this, she can get lost!

Cold runs the length of her, sharpening her mind as the danger penetrates further. *Lost. Yes... mercy! The scroll was right: this should not be a thing attempted by anyone but a true Master, because that which appears easy is, in fact, impossible without the strength and temperance to lift oneself from this dream-state once it's wrought! This... this was nothing like the brief Recall she managed in order to remember the instructions on the scroll, this... this was another level of... of discipline and command.*

Her own mistakes flaying, her ignorance so clear, Solancei almost pushed herself from the depth of these layers to escape. *She was aching everywhere, hurting... not a Master!*

Wild insight struck her that the person who called this thing to life had to be part of it: had to be in, had to ride the past like a spirit-with-no-body - just like the exercise of Recall demanded, but from there...?

A strong enough sense of wisdom was essential to create the 'Moment' - *and thus the 'Link'* - in the very blink that chance presented itself, but how did one recognise that? How did one consciously step outside time? How?

Anyone incapable of retaining true objectivity would simply lose focus. And to lose focus would be to 'linger'... and to linger would be to 'forget'... and to forget would be to... *to 'fade'.*

In a blast of heat, sudden panic ripped through her, turning her mind.

Something is keeping her down but she pushes hard to free herself and it yields.

Beating down terror with a cramped intake of air, Solancei flings her eyes open and hauls herself upright. The yielding 'thing' turns out to be the arm of Iambre's medic, who appears to have been leaning over her and now staggers under the half-pull, half-push of her patient. She must be used to such reactions though, because the woman manages to right herself - and for a moment, the medic's surcoat it is the whitest thing Solancei has ever seen: its heraldry of office - the branch and leaf - a simple vibrant green against all the pristine cleanliness.

Then her gaze escapes to find Wise-Lady Riselta's round blue eyes peering down into hers with a hint of anxiety and Solancei belatedly realises that the concern is directed at her. *What...?*

The medic carries herself whip-straight as ever and she is gaunt and tall; not quite skeletal but so tall that this close, Solancei has to crane her neck drastically to meet the other woman's eyes. The look she receives in return is patient and calm now. *It steadies her nerves though she does not let herself sink in deep, lest she forgets again...*

"Lady Solancei, How do you feel?" the medic's words carry the right mixture of concern and professional demand and with a mute nod of gratitude, Solancei drops her eyes and mumbles a brief 'thank you' as she lets go of Riselta's arm and manages not to stagger when left to test her balance.

She has only one thought riding her mind: the idea of calling the Moment Out of Time, and with her earlier weakness very much shadowing her with a warning of what will happen if she loses herself to the past again, she is suddenly filled with impatience. She does not care that she now finds herself on the far side of a fully erected camp, nor that she does not seem to belong here anymore - but she watches it all now, her mind alert; her eyes rowing, searching...

The medic pushes against her awareness. She is a portrait of scepticism. She appears to know that her patient is still upset and settles a hand against Solancei's neck, checking her pulse, then shifts it to her forehead, checking her temperature. Solancei barely notes the ministrations. The camp is laid out as the landscape permits, forming a rough pattern of three concentric rings, with the Princess' pavilions and officers' command tents set within the centre and the areas beyond made up of the crafts peoples' mobile workshops, the kitchen, the low tents of the mess, the communal habitats, the officers' tents and the wagons. The horse-lines and Iambre's carriage will usually be close to the main area of the second circle but Solancei cannot immediately spot either now, although she thinks she spies the outline of tents belonging to off-duty soldiers.

As it stands, it is not a large camp by any stretch of the imagination but it still looks as substantial as ever now that the surrounding area is full of the familiar spread of bleached linen canvasses designated the servants, and the stripes of black and green afforded the officers and advisers. The largest one - the one that looks like a small cottage and sports several compartments within - also flies the Ostravahn royal leopard from the central pole, and she wonders if Iambre has managed to wash away the dust with her usual cup of tea?

The idea draws her like a magnet and for a moment she is gripped by panic. *It seems so easy to get settled into the details; into the past. How will she do this now? What if she gets lost again?* She prays that she has not missed the right moment!

Wise-Lady Riselta tots under her breath, requiring her attention. Even in her fraught state of mind, she feels the medic's eyes on her; feels the woman's unvoiced question but she is too nervous of losing her mind again to even look at the medic. The heavy toll of hammers striking iron with an intermittent pattern of inflexible patience, echoes from nearby – a simple, everyday sound that calms her just about the same time as the medic reaches out and touches her shoulder. The contact makes her jump – she does not recall any of this ever happening before – but she also cannot quite find the calm to concentrate on what she thinks she must do and her attention is split between Riselta and sounds of the blacksmith's temporary workshop. Somehow she does not want Riselta's attention - as though she feels threatened that it too will draw her in - and she pulls away from the touch, stumbling until her back hits the wooden slats of a broad wagon parked up behind her.

In a blink, she realises that this is the farrier's vehicle: the one where she'd ended up when South-Point threw her – only this time she is bracing herself against the side of it rather than languishing on the trailer. *Would that be enough?*

"Lady Solancei,-" the medic intones in that solemn way of hers, one hand clamping around Solancei's bicep and breaking her thoughts, -you fainted. I think you got too hot. It would do you good to drink this."

Solancei looks down. With the suggestion, the woman foists a simple but vibrantly green-glazed crockery cup at her, its contents swilling - all but spilling. Solancei glances at it and though it has not got the clear aspect of water, the drink is nevertheless sweet smelling and suddenly very tempting. But she does not want to drink. The action will draw her too deeply back into the illusion, she fears, and she needs all of her wits to concentrate now so she shakes her head 'no'.

Why she is polite she does not know, she needn't be because none of this is real, but she declines the drink with an absent-minded smile regardless and begins to turn from the other woman, aware suddenly that her eyes are already working like a fluttering pair of hummingbirds, assessing, searching, looking... *all the while willing herself to find Klaas: to call a Link.*

Out of nowhere someone grips onto her; without a warning: tightening an arm around her neck and then she is suddenly struggling as she is drawn force-fully along the railings of the smith's wagon until her back bounces flush against the tall medic's chest. Riselta's arm fastens down tighter across Solancei's neck, strangling her near as. Somehow the scarf has been pulled low on her face, exposing her nose and mouth, and even as they struggle, the Wise-Woman's other hand manages to lifts the still-full beaker forth to force it against Solancei's lips.

"I said drink," she growls, in a voice unlike one Solancei's ever heard and the drink sloshes partly into her mouth, partly down her neck as the medic enforces her own command in a bewildering effort to see her patient drink the contents as ordered.

For a moment it almost works: the medic's brew hits Solancei's tongue and it is indeed sweet – sickeningly so – but she gags then, spewing out the contents like an exploding fountain between her lips. She is so utterly taken aback by this sudden onslaught, that she does not know whether to truly defend herself or simply relax and comply - and yet a part of her understands that she must be resisting with good reason.

For one, she does not recall this event at all, none of it; and her anger is slowing uncoiling – not the overpowering, mind-consuming type, but the cool distant kind that is enhanced by Veranto; the kind would have her defend herself with perfect awareness of everything that happens - and then she is moving. *Clasping the arm around her neck, twisting and dropping, weaving her own body under the grip of the medic's, she turns and ratchets Riselta's wrist the wrong way, snapping the bones like twigs as she repels the woman from contact. The medic curses like a man. This is all too weird!*

Solancei scrambles back. The thick-rimmed cup seems airborne for too long before it finally connects with the ground, its contents already flung from within. She struggles to keep her mind from splintering: it feels as though she has too much that needs to be thought about. The Wise-Lady Riselta is strangely out of place where she lies on the ground. She has fallen onto her front and Solancei cannot see her face – and though she hears the medic's gasps of pain they have a hollow, unreal quality to them, a thing that is emphasized by Riselta's surcoat, still a perfect white although the ground is loose enough to have sent Solancei's own boots dusty around the edges.

Everything about this strange assault is so completely out of character for the medic that a thought flickers in Solancei's mind that this is not really Riselta at all, but something other 'out of time' and the idea of such a possibility sends a myriad of imaginary insects marching down her spine.

Unnerved, she looks towards the smithy a mere twenty yards away. It semi-serves to break her own unease and gather her mind. No one has noted the small scrap, not even the handful of Metavo's men who appear to have assembled to pass the time by sharing various versions of a story about a dog, a pig and a prostitute.

Seeing them gives her a semblance of continuity for it is the story they told last time: when she'd been flat on her back in that very wagon next to her. On that day they'd been none the wiser to her presence either or else they would've probably curbed their vocabulary but now they carry on in her presence simply because it is part of the past she's called. Then, as now, the clipped sound of their Etruian accents make up for the tale's rudeness – and the story is sort of funny so she does not look for offence but all the same she cannot afford to get lost in the words of it either, for it would surely suck her intentions dry again.

She looks from the men to the medic, only to find the ground empty of both the Wise-Lady and the cup. Even the large satchel that Riselta carries everywhere has disappeared and if Solancei is not surprised, she is also not comforted. Calling a memory thus seems to carry far more hazards that she'd imagined – and now the chance to fashion the necessary Link seems to have passed her over yet again, this time not because she does not recall what she is doing here but because she's been distracted by the medic. *Somehow there is no irregularity to break the continuity now! Nothing!*

Not allowing her nuisance to grow, she loosens the ties of her veil and removes the fabric completely so that she can shake out her sweat-matted hair. That the medic had not tried to loosen it should've been a dead giveaway that all was not right but that is a lesson learnt. *So what now? Does she simply wait?*

Clasping the material of her veil, she pauses as though invited and leans one haunch against the dust-covered wheel of the flat-bottomed wagon. It has no awning now but she does not think it a big enough abnormality to attempt the Link. The rails of the tailgate are thrown down like before and with a glance, she thinks she sees the same spare anvil and tools still stored within. Ahead, under the farrier's open-sided tent that functions as his mobile workshop. The scene is a picture of busy normality: of two men working in the heat thrown off by fires hot enough to make the sweat trail like water from their temples and down their naked backs. The Captain's men have wisely placed themselves out of the immediate blaze radius. The latter share casual swigs from a communal water skin and they don't seem to begrudge the wait for their voices continue to rise and fall with the pleasant, but clipped accents of men born and raised in Etruia. It seems soothing. She knows they've seen her now, of course: she feels their eyes – and surprise – and understands it must be because of the veil. She ignores them and so they don't bother her, either. On or off, she supposes that such is still the 'power' of the veil - and though they are soldiers, they are still too well-versed in the Etruian ways to break with custom unless invited.

Solancei glances around and wipes the canvas-coloured excess of her un-dyed flaxen shirtsleeve across her forehead. She is dusty anyway; it doesn't matter that it comes away with a clay-coloured smear. She supposes she could try and create a moment out of nothing, rather than await another irregularity.

Might she be able to invite the men to speak with her? It does not seem viable somehow and she fears she does not pack the necessary training to make such a leap.

So you'll have to wait then, girl. Wait. And hope. And maybe even pray?

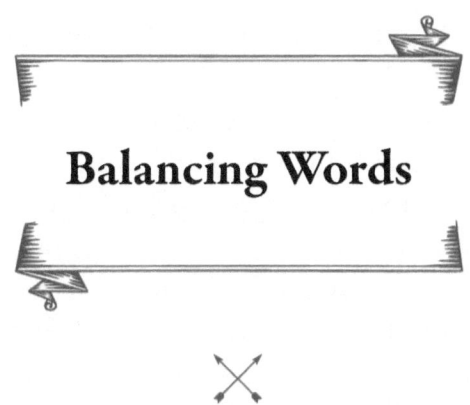

Balancing Words

ALONE WITH HIS THOUGHTS, Malandar shook himself free of the pressure that seemed to inhabit his mind. The dead reeked of more than blood and gore, the notion of affront against the Maker lingering, peppering the air with the potential of developing into something fouler that he did not wish to consider the ins and outs of right then. It both bound him to the spot and repelled him, but-

The First Guardian knew he had to move but somehow he couldn't, wishing once more that he could have dealt with these men all over again – or even better: not at all. It was odd to feel so... so haunted.

Though the memories of Richarmarlan Envalair had gone silent, new unease stole in like a shadow – a stray, almost indiscernible urge to check his surroundings for hidden foes: a warning, perhaps of things to come...

He raked a hand through his hair to clear it from his face and exhaled to punctuate the issue. Magic or no, he had to shake off this element of 'unbalance' that seemed to toy with his spirit. Black fell, but he felt as if he was losing himself every time the detachment wavered – which, since the long sleep, seemed a constant these days – and he needed to focus on his new task. Focus and plan. *Yet how did one plan for a Neidar Ba'raie?*

For a blink the First Guardian felt older than the Maker, unhitched from time and space, from gravity and life. The ground was under his feet, however. The emaciated power of the broken magic rode like a corrosive poison against skin and senses: this new reality rising to take him apart bit by bit, unless...

Malandar rolled his shoulders, inhaling just one deep breath.

Reality was never kind. For a moment he'd forgotten, but it never had been; never would be...

As if fading with his exhale, the feeling of unease unhitched itself, delivering him back to the world of monsters and strife. *His purpose here had not changed; a sliver of his former weariness lingered, like a tension along the backbone, but it couldn't matter.*

The idea of forging on re-acquainted him with something reminiscent of mortal discomfort, though; night was approaching; he'd not yet rested and his chances were diminishing by the moment, but he could not stay. The pollution of death hung too low in the air - the evidence of madness and failure weaving like an unknown spell, and even had he wanted to delay, his senses rebelled.

He had to leave – yet with the pace he'd been setting, he feared the horses would take him no further than a couple of leagues. It had to be enough though - and black fell, there it was again: the cursed reminder that this was not enough!

Exhaling softly this time, the First Guardian made himself look down one final time on the carnage he'd wrought. Apart from his 'digression', this was nothing but a stain in history; nothing in the face of what were to come and for a moment something coiled in him – a strange echo of his repressed Heritage that strained against the fact that he should be called to task over the ending of a few dirty lives. *This should not have been perceived a crime – the Maker should thank him...*

Malandar hitched a staggered breath, his senses spinning as the hard, disloyal thought bore into him like a parasite. For a blink wondering where the hex he was, weariness washed through him, shunting his balance, leaving him slightly fevered and spent - just as he was want to feel after each time the Veils had been successfully restored and he'd been depleted of most of his strength. *But what for? So much gone; so much changed; still a long way... still a long, long way to go!*

Feeble realisation almost drowning before he could catch it to twist some meaning from it, he recognised that the memories mixed with the scent of blood and dirt were making him tense again. There'd been so much loss over the aeons that it was barely sane to think about – and still it went on. *But perhaps -* Malandar rolled his neck and consciously relaxed his muscles with another quiet sigh – *Perhaps, it would only truly End on the day the Mad Ones stood victori-*

ous atop the ashes of the crumbled Realms, toasting Chaos in the skull cups of dead Guardians...

Malandar knew these dark thoughts a sarcastic reminder of the person he'd left behind on the day of his Rebirth and this awareness helped centre his sense of purpose and re-adjust his equilibrium. *If the Mad Ones toasted victory, vengeance would be forfeit and that was an inconceivable outcome; consequences of meddling aside: his theory on the use of a Neidar Ba'raie must work to become fact! It must!*

Trying not to breathe in too deeply, Malandar looked upon the dead men a moment longer and knew a sense of loathing – both for the way this place already stank like an abattoir as well as for Silicia'Cha's beguiling ways - but done was done, and grimacing with the need, the First Guardian swiped back the tails of his long-coat and began to extricate himself from the 'ring of death' with a series of carefully-placed steps.

The Vessel had drenched the ground in a widening but already congealing pool of dark fluids that had reached to soak into the forms of the men who'd fallen closest, but even though it was without a doubt a trial on the senses, it was once more the simple ugliness of life-wasted that offended the most. Stray urges aside, Malandar still had ethics beyond those that bound him through the Laws of Existence and he couldn't help but draw a cleansing breath when his one final stride saw him safely beyond the patch occupied by slain renegades. Like the three men he'd sent scampering, he did not look back as he began to reverse his steps along his original path - back towards the horses – and he was pleased when he could finally leap across the heinar and then the rock to duck through the natural fence.

'... -Guardian Commander! Speak to me! First Guardian?!'

Out of nowhere, Thessilia Emara's voice crackled alive inside his head - for the second time this eve disturbing his thoughts with question and uncertainty - and at that moment he belatedly recalled how he'd cut her off earlier, nearly as ruthlessly as he'd disposed of Silicia'Cha's Vessel.

He'd quite likely kept her rudely shut-out from the events that had followed and knowing Guardian Emara as he did, she'd would've been hammering against his sealed mind with an increasing sense of alarm whilst he'd fought *the Elated* and had continued to ignore her. It was another thing poorly done and by now the lady might possibly be quite furious...

"Wrath and Bones, Commander Denarlin, speak to me, I—'

'Emara, I am here,' he cut in, suddenly acerbic for no reason, *'Stop barraging me with noise!'*

'Hah, drivel! If you don't like my tone, then answer me! No better still: don't just cut me off like I am of no concern! Pray tell: what the high prancing prick was that!?'

Feeling ill-touched all over again, Malandar expelled a breath like a hiss and felt his equilibrium flex.

'Vermin!' he told her with a grimace, lengthening his stride across the uneven ground as though he might outpace all memories of the event but with his next step disturbing a dark-mottled rorka adder from sleep. As though on cue, the narrow-tailed venomous worm flared its double fangs at him in displeasure, the pincer at the end of its tapering body riding suddenly high and ready to deliver either death or euphoria. *Almost he wished it would hit him with a dose of adrenaline; almost...*

Malandar spat at the indignant creature and the sly predator wavered, retracting its tail as though acceding room to a larger cousin.

'Vermin?' Thessilia Emara repeated flatly, pulling his attention from the rorka. She sounded taken aback but as she spoke next, a sliver of suspicion crept into her words, *'So? You deliberately cut me off for 'vermin'? Hmm, Guardian Denarlin, either you are slowly misplacing your mind amongst the stars somewhere or your are—'*

'I was attacked by a Vessel and his motley crew of fools.' Malandar injected curtly, his now more or less permanent frown as vexing as an unexpected autumn chill. *'I was a little unprepared. It's dealt with. Now what were you telling me when we were so crudely interrupted?'*

But Thessilia wasn't going to leave it so neatly; he felt her professional alarm spike almost immediately at his shortened words and then she was at him, her mind and presence burrowing in around his like a second skin, searching, concerned: just on the cusp of invading.

'Guardian Emara, refrain!' he ordered, the words silky and sharp as he cut through her clamouring with the command of obedience linked directly to his Power as First Guardian.

Though he should've been pleased, it was suddenly a questionable pleasure to feel Alérathnar's hand still working for him and through him. Thessilia retreated in an instant and it left behind an echo of her intent - sweet with concern, smoky from his denial - and as usual, it made him recall that she was not intentionally seeking to raise his ill will; not like Mehand'Arun, or Utarion, even.

'Now that was uncalled for, General!' she whispered with aloof affront that sounded like sheaves of ripened wheat rustling in the back of his mind. It reminded him in a blink of Marlan's ghostly voice for she was suddenly so far away that he could barely feel her, let alone hold onto their connection, but if he didn't, however, there'd be more questions to answer. And still...

It was by little skill and sheer determination that he somehow managed to reach the horses *and* retain a hold on their link without mishap for the effort left him nothing spare other than a hairline of awareness as to where his next step should fall. Thessilia rarely sulked, but with her self-imposed distance, he thought she came remarkably close now and she gave him no help. It made him feel, yet again, like a First-Tier Apprentice: without a clue and with no strength of mind to diversify his power - *black hex, no sooner had he rekindled a belief in the Maker's power and then it was gone again; and how had he forgotten that Thessilia could be stubborn beyond recourse?*

Pausing to rub Ghost's long forehead in response to the horse's questing nuzzle as he drew up next to it, Malandar noted that thankfully the animals did not appear too upset by the events that had taken place a mere stone's throw away; they'd been grazing down-wind and he thanked that cold sweeping breeze now for clearing the air with every step that removed him from the dead.

'You were pushing me, Guardian,' he offered her then as a way of smoothing matters out, though of course he didn't have to, *'I will not apologise—'* Thessilia sent him a spike of very un-Guardian-like 'see-if-I-care' but Malandar ignored her, *'—but neither should you! I have, however, been pushed around enough for one night and I suppose...*

"Well I suppose, I feel a little short of good-will right now. There are six dead men cresting the ground I just occupied – one of them Silicia'Cha's Vessel no-less and now I have to forge on, though the Maker knows my horses are already foot-sore enough to reverse what weak advance I've achieved!'

'Dead men? You killed them?' Thessilia quested a little too quickly, slightly breathless with question and already beyond slight. He suspected she'd per-

formed her small routine of 'hurt-female' quite deliberately - and to a tee, at that – just in order to get him to talk but he suddenly didn't mind.

'*But how come, Commander?*' she puzzled. '*You feel this was justified?*'

'*Oh there was little choice in the matter,*' Malandar admitted, feeling the oppressive absence of magic suddenly press in on him from all directions, '*and you forget that the magic is unreliable. Justified or not, they were touched by the Mad Ones; they were raising steel against me! Black fell, I am still the First Guardian!*'

He paused before he could spin further half-truths, then told her, '*As it were I sent three of them running without memory, but all of them ready to praise the Maker. What would you have suggested I do? Let them hustle me? Let them incapacitate my person as though I were the criminal?*'

'*No but—*'

'*Guardian Emara, Guardian Orleara is the ancient Sunerai citizen amongst us, by which token I'd expect her the one most likely to protest against any violence committed... but you? Let it rest and trust me... today of all days, I'd be the first to agree with such sentiment and yet it is done!*'

'*Yet what-*'

'*If you think to speak on behalf of our pacifist colleague so as to raise a compelling case for my mistake, then do so later but for now, let's not waste time. I already recognize certain errors of my conduct and that is my fault to bear.*'

'*Fine, very well,*' she relented, '*but I'd still like to know what you are not telling me, Commander!*'

Leaning slightly against the horse, Malandar killed a sigh. '*I am not telling you what I cannot yet explain; suffice it to inform you that the bastard Vessel put a blade to my throat and that it was... unexpected!*'

Pause... wherein he felt Thessilia's incredulity momentarily swamp her ability to think. He knew what must be going through her mind. No one ever laid a sword to his throat.

'*So Silicia'Cha you say?*' she said then, smoothly pirouetting from the subject, wisely sensing that she should ask for no further details even if a number of questions were clearly playing havoc with her mind. '*You didn't get any blood on you now, did you?*'

'*Guardian Emara, please! How can you ask?*' He berated, though knowing she was bartering for time to recover.

'Hmm, good and well then... but tell me: did the crazy hussy recognize you? Perhaps that would not be so bad? If they know of your presence then surely you could call Ambar'Zadron to your side and be upon the Tarvia within what...? The day?'

Malandar offered the horizon a ghost of a smile for her easy logic, left the grey and went to busy himself with the other two.

'Surely?' he stabbed as he began to make preparations for his departure. *'Thessilia Emara kindly leave off that annoyingly Human way you have of making too many assumptions in any one go! In regards to Ambar'Zadron, you'll be pleased to know that you tempt my need immensely to make it so. And yet I hardly think it the best strategy to abandon all sense and let the whole realm of enemies know exactly where I am. No matter what, I am not equipped to fight a host of Vessels on my way to the Tarvia - and let me assure you that this is exactly what we'd have to face. Perhaps... perhaps, if the Black Eyed Army was already at our disposal, but—'*

Malandar cut himself off and changed direction as he moved around and reached down to feel the bay's cannon bone and pastern, finishing with an inspection of the hoof before moving onto the next leg in order to repeat the procedure. For a few moments he remained quiet, busying himself with the simple task of checking the horses, and Thessilia gifted him with mental space to do so, perhaps stealing time to organise her own thoughts, but displaying an admirable show of patience that he himself seemed to lack. *It couldn't be helped though.*

Returning to Ghost, he let the silence grow heavy as his he worked, allowing his inspection to draw onto Layliana before choosing to rekindle conversation.

'Silicia'Cha knows of my presence,' he admitted then, *'but this landscape is vast: she will not be able to predict my path and she will not be able to find me easily, even with the aid of another Vessel. Without the Eikyr, I am just another traveller and stealth is still to our advantage, even if I shall endeavour to ensure it will only be for a short while longer – and then...*

'Well, then I will hopefully not care if the whole host of Mad Ones knows where I am or what I do.'

'Hmm... You sound confident. Does that mean then that you have found some of the lost artefacts? Does this mean that you might finally get around to sharing

that plan of yours with the rest of us? The Speaker wishes to know about this theory you mentioned, just as he wishes to learn: how goes your search? I am of course inclined to tell him to ask you himself but since there appear to be problems reaching across, I'd be happy to pass on news – in whatever shape it might take. Indeed, I do as a matter of fact feel obliged to warn you that he should be greatly heartened at this point to hear of any kind of breakthrough.'

'As should we all,' Malandar *injected darkly, 'but for now you can tell the Speaker what you see fit; tell him I may only be days away from finding a reliable way of contacting him - but also explain that I am uncertain as to the success of this venture for there is a certain level of risk involved, not to mention the possibility that it might not work.'*

For a moment Thessilia's attention peaked again, but she managed to keep her curiosity under tight restraint then as she inclined her chin, allowing him to continue.

'Now as for the Speaker?' he enquired, *'You have news, you said? And what about yourself? What have the Elvern to say about the broken flows?'*

'Oh yes... the flows... the Elvern... well, they say precious little, I'm afraid; broken flows or not, the Elvern are as stubborn as ever-,' Thessilia smiled tightly, *'-and predictably they insist that they have no problems and that matters are fully under control. I know that they are re-inventing the truth of course, but conditions are acceptable and I feel that they have spent the last thousand years telling themselves that everything is fine so that's the way of the land, even if certain spells have been proven to go awry. However, make no mistake: underneath all the posturing they are scared. They hide it well but all is not sound in the kingdom, I fear, and I suspect they are reluctant to share because they will be forced to face the problem.'*

Thessilia broke off a moment as her frustration blossomed, but then she brightened considerably, *'Oh, but on the amusing side: did I tell you that they still remain in uproar over the fact that Guardian Mehand'Arun has been forced into 'serving' the Speaker? Oh and how it rankles that they have thus been left with 'a mere Human' like myself to tend their borders?'*

Thessilia shivered as if she was trying to rid herself of a bad thought – and failed, *'Uh, by the Maker, how I abhor this one-way diplomacy! I swear to you that were I not a Guardian, they'd have kicked me straight out of New Verranor just thirty of their ruddy minutes upon arrival! Good thing I thrive on rubbing myself the right way up their silken skin, so to speak.'*

Malandar got a quick impression of Thessilia's wry view of the situation through a series of impressions flittering through her mind, but if anyone could walk this line, it was Emara. The Elvern would never dare threaten one of the Upper Circle; not openly, but there were other ways of making a representative's life... *trying.*

The First Guardian let a touch of understanding seep down the bond but to doubt her ability to deal with this, was to doubt the Maker's choice. And Malandar did not question either. The female Guardian had the patience of a saint, along with the vocabulary of an Ermaron tribal commander, and she had a way of studying a person, a way of finding out all the small private things, which no one else supposedly knew! It made her not only a skilled diplomat but also an expert in the use of verbal slights and veiled insults, and should the need arise, Malandar had no doubt that she would be well-armoured to handle any given situation. His father's people were 'tricky'. Thessilia Emara would thrive on this - at least for a short while until she got bored or someone important had had their fill and began throwing insults and challenges...

'Recall that the magic still flows in Heirah-Noor, Guardian,' Malandar stated as a tart reminder then, and warned, *'Kindly see to it that you do not kill anyone!'*

'Ah unlike you, you mean?' She quipped, but Malandar grimaced and she fell back in line.

'But I am a Guardian of the Upper Circle, am I not?' she said, seriousness pooling. *'There will be no such occasion, I assure you. Even the Elvern would not dare provoke me to such action, as well you know. There are insults and then there are Insults. Their own would rise against any such protagonist faster than an Eikyr lashes its tail; certainly, you have not been to your old 'home' in a blessedly long time but things don't change around here - again, you of all people know this.'*

He shrugged guilelessly, but she spoke the truth. *He knew all about it and more...*

Feeling Thessilia about to speak other tart words, he kept himself carefully neutral, hoping she'd refrain. The Elvern people were not the only race of Dallancea to possess flaws, but theirs were many. Now, however, was not the time to 'reminisce', and his silence seemed to do the trick, for Thessilia swallowed what might have been on her mind in favour – he felt – of safer issues.

'Anyway, on a different note, the very useful thing is, that in spite of all their posturing and fronting, I am reliably certain that I can leave their high-handed

Hunters to control matters for a time whilst I look to the west.' Thessilia sounded only a little vexed now. *'Good grief, Commander, the foul people don't want me here anyway and I don't truly want to stay though obligation would keep me, of course, so perhaps-*

'Well that is to say: since we have time, my presence will perhaps count better towards aiding your quest? You have told me to call together the Black Eyed Army. In the light of the Elvern claim to independence, I don't see why I should not press on and strive to oblige your request sooner rather than later. In fact, Alérathnar willing, I should be able to Chase the Horizon in less than ten Ostravahn days. Now would this be a satisfactorily time-frame with which to work?'

'Do as you must. Ten days are better than the current forecast,' Malandar encouraged, keeping to himself how much he would have preferred her to halve that time. They'd Quickened early, yes – but somehow the benefit of time seemed to be slipping right through their fingers.

With the risk of sounding overly much like the Speaker, he added, *'Of course you must be assured of the Elvern People's persuasion in this before we can oblige them – and ourselves. Make King Ashtar'Naahvan swear it so and we can move. Otherwise, do not leave. I suggest you try and get the King's word as soon as you may, then do your best to lay your time and presence where it is better needed. And wanted.'*

'Understood Commander.' Guardian Emara affirmed, her blade-like smile not escaping his notice though she worked to keep her pleasure under control. He only hoped that Ashtar'Naahvan would oblige; the King might not welcome Emara's presence any more than any of his Councillors, Weavers, or Hunters, but that did not mean he did not see the prudence, regardless. *Thessilia might yet be going nowhere...*

The Final Card

A SIZZLING HISS OF water interrupts upon her calm.

Solancei looks back at the smithy just as a cloud of steam rises from one of the water buckets used to quench the iron. It's the stocky, sandy-haired apprentice who has completed yet another horseshoe, she sees, as he hauls the item back out with a pair of giant-sized tongues. This one is a large oval, the size of both her hands put together and she spies the tang of burnt nails in the air then, a reminder of the work that has gone into the preparation to ensure that the finished product will fit Cook's enormous draught horse. *It is all still as she remembers...*

Above, a lark sings just like last time and Solancei feels herself sway. *I must be mad... what if I can't do this? What if I really cannot do this?!*

The relentless banging of the hammer against steel and the sizzling sound that accompanies every dip of hot metal into the water trough is like tiresome music in the now-otherwise quiet camp and time seems to fluctuate. Cook's horse is led away, then two other: Iambre's Arrow, Guards-Man Elar's grey Kaldun – all in the same order as before. Second-in-Command Kimonar's borrowed Rayon will be next. The black is a handsome stallion, its sleek coat shining near blue under the sun as it moves as directed by the apprentice, head perked and ears twisting. For a full-blooded stallion, it is polite.

Oddly, the horse suits its temporary owner well, she reflects – a thought she has no reason to retract when - as though on cue - Captain Metavo's Lieutenant chooses that very moment to stroll past on the opposite side of the open wagon. With a grimace of sympathetic camaraderie, Kimonar offers her a crooked smile over the vehicle's raised sidebars but does not pause to engage in conversation. Instead, he heads for the black and pats the animal without comment or further interaction; she is well aware, however, just how he raises and keeps his all-too blue eyes on her just a moment too long. *Eyes all for her, as he continues to stroke the Rayon's dark flanks.*

Solancei looks away, uncertain what to think. When she dares look back up, his attention has gone elsewhere but she knows that when she returns her eyes to the farrier, she'll catch him looking again. It will be nothing more than a quick flash probably; by the sounds of the hails, he is now making his way across to the remaining three men in order to join their conversation - this one about the ethics of honouring wagers. *But he'll definitely glance at her. Because he always does.*

Solancei hides a woeful smile and wishes she'd never removed the veil. Not that she cares in that way, but she has already known for a while that he likes her - and her hair *is* a bold mess. In turn, she supposes that Kimonar del'Draventar is easy to like and perchance his interest goes a little deeper than simply 'liking' as well - a silly notion that both Ina and Iambre have commented on several times already. So far, however, she has shot down their enthusiastic comments whenever she's overheard them. It has been a long time since anyone has liked her *like that,* and the possibility of someone thinking of her in such a way does not seem quite real to her – not even if it certainly would go a long way in explaining why Kimonar never seems too fazed by her often spiky temper. *Gods but the man doesn't even appear to feel uncomfortable when I look at him and instead it is he who makes me uncomfortable. What a change!*

For a moment she allows herself to consider the prospect and it might not be too much of a hardship, she allows: Kimonar is easy company, courteous, polite – *yes, nice even.* He is a noble like herself: so no complications about stations clashing, and – *unbelievably* - he has been known to make her laugh, too!

Solancei feels the corner of her mouth move in a tiny smile at the thought. Somehow Kimonar knows not to mollycoddle her; somehow he knows how to walk the line between propriety and good-natured cheek, and he is a damned good soldier too: she's watched him train, seen him move. Still... she fears that if she were to give Iambre just half an inclination that she does not dislike the fellar, her friend will be delighted. Sadly, she also knows that it'll be the kind of delight that will see Iambre throw her right into the man's open arms, which - *when all is said and done* - is not where she wants to be.

Solancei kills the smile. Lieutenant del'Draventar is... *agreeable*... but quite unlike Iambre, she is not in love and the idea of 'tangling laces' - *as Klaas would call it* - does not figure on her agenda. She is not really forbidden or anything like that, but she knows full-well how rumours can spread: like a disease and with barely much effort either, and she will not clear the path for such seeds to grow again! However, it reaches even deeper than that! Gods but even if she is not 'haunted' by certain unfortunate past events, there are still a hundred other reasons why any kind of 'messing around' is nigh-on unthinkable to her. She is not prudish like Palea nor is she too craven to try, no - but she's long since made herself a wow that it'll take more than a title and a handsome pair of eyes to catch her out again and she intends to stand by her decision. *And besides: someone around here has to keep a clear head!* So let Iambre suffer the effects of her foolish infatuation with Captain Metavo - *if she will not wise up, she stands to get burnt* – but Solancei has no time for 'casual acquaintances', easy company or no!

She folds her arms across the chest and deliberately shifts her body slightly to remove the group of men from sight. Instead, she looks out on the camp, hoping that by some chance, she'll feel inspired not to believe herself a fool for lingering here. In honour of the hot weather, the retainers are in full vigour erecting several trestle tables and folding chairs directly outside the five 'command' pavilions and Solancei studies the hive of activity without much interest, casually noticing Metavo emerge from one colourful tent, clearly with the intentions of abducting an armful of large scrolls. *Maps,* she guesses, *to help plot the next leg of their route. Poor man! Bet he'd simply love to wring a different path right out of thin air too...*

Solancei pauses, a sudden vibe gripping her. *A different path...?*

In the next blink, understanding hits her.

Like someone suddenly swipes clear her head, she sees that all of this... *her actually standing here and not lying on the body of the farrier's wagon... that her entire, whole day since not falling off South-Point... that it is all...*

She swallows... *that this is all one huge abnormality! Like one extraordinary deviant from that original day... all rolled into one!*

It sends her heartbeat thumping, pins scratching down her spine like tiny icicles. *Dear Gods! Fleck! Will it really be that simple? Could it be?*

It happens in a flash but suddenly it is as though her mind can concentrate on nothing else but Klaas! The name, her voice, the feel of her presence, the way she moves, the way she is: it simply spills into her head till she has no choice but to close her eyes – or maybe she doesn't; she no longer knows – but she lets the feeling take her down, the insistent need growing... expanding...

The world wavers... *a ripple across a dream of reality and then...*

" ...but they will have a different idea, no doubt-" the clipped voice reaches her first, "-so when you have completed the rounds of Flee Lane, scan through Low Scar and Tanners' walk. Connect with Dromund at the docks, we'll need to make this speedy."

The instructions make no sense but the voice does. Klaas!

Too amazed, lightning seems to strike understanding inside her body then, and her eyes fly open just as her head whips towards the clear sound of the Chief's all-too-familiar cadence. *Her mentor is not yet back in camp.* She knows this rationally and yet somehow Klaas is right here anyway; exactly where she needs to be - *mercy, as if called!*

And then the voice is no longer just a voice. Solancei sees her then: amidst an oddly fussy void that seems to be part of a dream, yet also very much real because the image of Klaas Mehadja is suddenly much sharper than the rest of the hazy, out-of-focus life in Iambre's camp. *And it is getting clearer... solidifying...*

"-and so we will see what-" while she speaks, her mentor looks up, almost casually, dark eyes coming to focus, then widens.

In a whisper of a blink, the intended words seem to die on the older woman's lips; *forgotten...*

For a moment, her mentor hovers thus, without moving, frozen, oblivious to her surroundings, then Klaas blinks. *A slewed, deliberate action, as though controlled and willed by great effort.*

Klaas blinks again.

Solancei doesn't move. She's too stunned. In utter synchronicity, their eyes seem to meet over the short distance separating them – a mere ten feet of dry ground, yet so much more – and as Solancei looks into her mentor's wide gaze, she sees the old woman blink again, her countenance one of growing shock, but-.

Little by little, a feeling close to euphoria begins to envelop her. *She's done it! She's used the Moment Out of Time and forged a Link! Holy teeth and-*

For a heartbeat Solancei struggles to breathe as the enormity of her achievement hits her, then she shakes herself. *The Knights Commander! Iambre!* She cannot linger on her triumph! *Tell Klaas... Tell...!*

The length of veil she's been twisting into a rope of sorts, falls from her stiff fingers, but she doesn't notice. It is not real, nor is her presence here, or the camp, or-

A pain in her head suddenly immobilises her. It's like a hedgehog of nails that is slowly being forced into her skull by an invisible hand! It comes with no warning - and causes Klaas' appearance to waver in and out of focus as though her eyes are now failing to make sense of this picture within a picture. Mercy, but it will not do!

Taking action, Solancei expelled her entire breath in a sharp gush as if someone had rammed a fist into her guts, and somehow managed to stabilise the Link although the headache did not entirely desist. Without delay, she reached for Klaas as the woman solidified once more: *reached hand and mind as if she'd been thrown a lifeline and now sought to grab a hold of it before she went under for the last time. Gods, it was hard...*

Suddenly shaking with the strain of maintaining her position here, Solancei knew she did not have long - yet Klaas did not move, did not appear as if she even could, as she stood there, one hand half-lifted and whatever gesture she'd been about to make seemingly forgotten along with the words that belonged to a conversation of another time and place. *Fleck!*

For a moment Solancei thought she was fighting a losing battle as her own strength seemed to drop from under her so rapidly that she collapsed to her knees as the exercise continued to drain her. *She could not do this alone! She needed Klaas' help, but did Klaas even see her? Gods, but she had to make her see her!*

The strain of *reaching* was weighing her down like a hundred shackles attached around her every limb, and it was making it hard for her to retain her mentor in focus, but she fought on doggedly till she managed to claw back upright, using the spokes of the wagon wheel for support. Eyes on Klaas, she forced her feet to take one shuffling step forward, then another. *The Chief had to see her! She had to!* She had no idea what would happen if she actually *touched* Klaas through the Link – it might just blow her efforts sky high or it might burn-out her ability or it might not even be possible to connect 'physically' as well as mentally – and still she stumbled on, another step, desperately hoping that her mentor would respond or give off some indication that this was not just some crooked dream after all!

The Chief, meanwhile, remained frozen mid-move – her blunt surprise evident in every line of her face even as a dawning look of incredulity began to spread across her tight features. Seemingly speechless, she looked Solancei directly in the eye, but it was not good enough! *Focus here Klaas, Gods damn you, focus! Help me!*

Solancei was close enough now – *or should that be invested enough?* – to see a large man swaddled in the dark directly at Klaas' right shoulder, however, he did not appear to notice that the Chief's attention had swivelled elsewhere. Instead, he simply offered her mentor a brief nod of assent before he drew away from what Solancei now understood must be a tavern table with four dull-gleaming pewter cups and a few spluttering candles sitting randomly on top. She opened her mouth to speak... somehow she felt her lips move but the words didn't project as they should and icy despair filled her. *She'd come so far but she couldn't do this... she'd fail!*

'Klaas, help!" she whispered, barely loud enough for her own ears to hear, but she was drained.

The Chief still never blinked. Slowly, ever so slowly, however, her mentor lowered her forgotten hand back to the table as though to brace herself. An inhale followed; Solancei saw her chest rise...

"Lancei?" The Chief questioned then, her pronunciation deliberately slanted towards incredulous question and her sustained disbelief pulling to smooth certain lines of her hard-cut features whilst accentuating others.

"Lancei?" Klaas repeated, more firmly now, a spark of feeling entering her voice, "Good Gods... girl, are you...? Are you Soul Reaching?!"

For a moment Solancei could not speak nor move. Quite as though she also needed support, the Chief kept her hands planted squarely on the trestle as her chin dipped minutely to offer Solancei a pained look past the bridge of her brow.

Though Klaas was shrouded by the pervasive semi-darkness of the tavern's insides, Solancei could see her mentor's face beginning to pale...

Unseated by the sight, she braced herself. It was not even a surprise to Solancei to see the breadth of dark disapproval in her mentor's gaze now. *It had been expected.*

As though in search of strength, Klaas looked away, rocking forward a little, seemingly in contemplation of the situation. *Come on...*

For a beat, the older woman looked about to say something more, but instead - with an enormous crash that would've made anyone in close vicinity jump out of their skins - the Chief pounded a fist into the table hard enough to bounce the pewter and set candle flames swaying.

A blazing look of anger scorching Solancei's mind, the Chief's sudden emotion seemed to solidify the Link as she finally lifted wrath-hazed eyes to her 'disobedient student' and grated, "Allziu'Chi's Teeth, girl! Is this a jest?! Do you know what you are doing?! Do recognise the danger?! Do you?!"

Though Klaas was only short of stature and slight in body, her mind was awesome and her aura fearsome. *For this Solancei would have the Void to pay – and still, she'd gladly pay whatever the Chief wanted, if only the older woman would help her now!*

Rather than shrinking from her mentor's anger, Solancei felt the quiver of a smile lift the corners of her mouth and for a moment she was so light-headed with relief, she could've fainted.

"Klaas! You see me!" she blurted, her voice oddly shaky, "You actually see me then? Gods... the Spirit Reach works. It works!"

Emotions rolling high but gathering her faculties, Solancei focused her mind on what needed saying, "Klaas... please... I have not much time: but you are all in danger! I cannot relay details but beware of the-"

The hissing of fiery metal entering water cut through her words, halting her thoughts. When she did not concentrate on Klaas, her world did not seem to have stopped spinning yet and it made her sway on her feet. She'd found Eso, yes! But everything else was still there, like a dream within a dream which made it hard for her to keep her focus in one place. *Something appeared to pick at the periphery; at the stitches of her attention... something she might not want to know...*

Behind Klaas' suddenly-opaque presence, she saw the farrier thrust a half-finished oval of iron back into the hot fire, digging it in and working up the embers and heat until cinders flew like fireflies and Solancei imagined that she could feel the blaze intensify. It made her think that something was not right... something similar to the incident with the medic: a sixth sense of sorts... and then her flesh began to crawl.

Wrong! Something was wrong!

It was all she had time to think... *crawling flesh... wrong!* Next, the harsh smell of smoke and burning skin hit her nostrils sharply, just as all sound cut off and her entire world began to waver – this time, all around her. Then the past she'd 'Called' began collapsing, as did the Link. She felt the deterioration of her concentration like fine splinters flying off a larger piece of wood worked by the wrong tool, the damage irreversible, and-

No! Flecking no!

Her eyes veered back to Klaas in alarm, widening with fear now, and she saw her mentor throw out a hand towards her then - without reserve or recrimination now. *'Help me',* she thought, and suddenly Klaas appeared to fight the 'collapse' from her end too.

The hard frown cutting her mentor's forehead, altered. Brought to bear from the strain of new focus now, Klaas' drawn look revealed a sudden gritty aspect of alarm that the Chief would not normally have allowed anyone to see because it betrayed a weakness.

The show of such naked emotion almost floored Solancei, but for a few heartbeats she also took hope as Klaas ascetic features twisted into a ferocious mask of concentration...

Yet the splinters became a blizzard. Klaas was shouting something, but the words were drowned, distance widening, silence screaming...

An odd void pulling her backwards, Solancei's perception shifted. Then she was floating, suspended, light yet heavy. Through a haze, she saw her mentor slide from view, then re-solidify. The re-established collection strayed knife sharp for a beat, but maybe Klaas was too late, or not strong enough – or indeed, maybe it was Solancei who was not strong enough – then, suddenly, bewilderingly, everything around her: Klaas, the smithy, the soldiers, the ground and the dry landscape... *like an image of smoke and mirrors it all dissolved, ceasing to be.*

A crushing weight filled her. In the place of her earlier construct, only meandering tendrils of sharp smoke prevail: intense now because it was all there was in a world turned dark; in a world without place or centre.

An illusion, this too lasted but a blink, and then - like shards of broken glass swept away by a housekeeper's persistent broom – she was left, not battling dry dust or a hot autumn sun, but with the overpowering need to retch or gag or both. A noxious, rancid smell of charred flesh burned her nostrils, coating the back of her throat.

For a beat longer, the heavy feeling dragged at her, then released.

As though returning to the surface of her imaginary lake after a deep dive, she sliced through the layers of Veranto gasping for breath, then came round, the urgent feeling of wrongness spreading deeper, demanding attention: urging her to pull back into the physical confines of the body she'd somehow forgotten herself still attached to. It was somehow a monstrous idea. There was peril awaiting her there. She knew she didn't want to go back, yet a lurching pull ripped her forward regardless. *Fear followed, hollowing and dry...*

Arriving back to consciousness in the very instant danger appeared to snap real teeth at her, her eyes flew open of their own accord in time with the first conscious, ragged breath entering her lungs. *It felt odd. Strangely laborious.* But then the sense of time re-enveloped her and as the fumes in the air made her cough, the next ragged breath automatically raked in and out of her lungs, hurting as if it was a forced thing: not natural... *burning...*

Utterly disorientated, Solancei tried to move, but couldn't. Like she'd regressed into a bad dream, she belatedly recalled she was still immobilised on the rack, yet the clammy sense of 'wrongness' persisted, adding confusion. *The frigid air reeked: the smoky drag at her lungs too laboured; too unwholesome.*

She coughed hard.

The horror of ignorance and displacement speed through her like random shots of venom - then the clarity of her failure struck home. Taunting. *Klaas... she'd lost the Link...*

It turned her core a blazing sub-zero in a flash, and her spirit even colder. *No dear Gods... no...*

A near-sob escaped her as she closed her eyes and saw again Klaas' desperate face as she tried to steady the Link - finally aiding her student regardless of personal conflict.

In response, her world spun again, the rapid change not yet fully registered with her body, and the displacement-

Sickened to the core with vertigo, she retched, suddenly overcome with physical illness as she became truly aware of the taste in her mouth and the smell in the cell.

Turning her face, not bothered about refinement, she spat out the remnants of some oily liquid from her mouth. Her chin, already wet with some equally sweet-smelling stickiness that had somehow spilt down her neck and across her shoulder, was another thing that didn't belong but her mind was still too distracted by the acidic smoke in the air to pay this much heed. *The world would not keep still...*

She retched again. The tendrils of smoke caught the back of her throat, but she fought the cough. Like a shot of energy she'd normally converge into something useful, fear raced along her spine, and she spat again, the taste in her mouth horrendous, like rancid honey overlaying foreign herbs, her mind not quite knitting together what she already knew in her subconscious to be true, yet didn't have the words to quantify, and Klaas... *Merciful Gods, she'd failed!*

Again she coughed, her eyes watering from the exposure to the smoke-polluted air, her throat continuing to burn in strange opposition to the sweet taste in her mouth and it pulled another retching cough from her, her mind solidifying a little more in the present with every laboured beat of her erratic pulse. *She'd failed...*

Sick to the core, drenched in strange exhaustion, her deficiency cut. *She'd come so close. Close enough to touch Klaas! Close enough to warn her-*

For a moment Solancei wanted to weep as her insides seemed to crumble like a cliff, long-suffering erosion. *And Iambre...*

"I am relieved to have you back with us, grey-eyes. Truly, it'll take no genius to acknowledge that we nearly lost you there!"

Drawn abruptly from internal misery, she raised her eyes to the man she'd momentarily pushed from existence. In direct line of vision, the Knights Commander did not move, yet it took her a moment to recognize him through the gauzy atmosphere. *Her head refused to cooperate.* The spinning continued: a slow belligerent sensation that eroded her ability to form a connection between a length of metal in the Knight Commander's hand and his odd pose near her left thigh.

She blinked, eyes still watering as they followed the obese tendrils of smoke slowly migrate upwards: reforming, then lazily dissipating under the low ceiling with a near-sentient reluctance. *The stench seemed permanent; everything wrong.*

She swallowed bile but the spinning sensation was finally subsiding enough to allow her head to recover, and after a couple of heartbeats her mind finally formed the right picture with 'the everything wrong' that trapped her.

Someone gasped like they'd just been punched - a soft explosion of sound riding the event; the pause before the rush of their next intake of air too excruciating as the rhythm of each subsequent half-formed inhale and exhale was rent hard from their body as though they couldn't catch their breath fast enough for relief; as though the pain raked high enough to raise panic.

But the sound was not coming off anybody else. It was emanating from her!

A surge of emotion cut past the Veranto, her breath hick-upping in her lungs, drenching her in urgency, but she remained trapped, and Zulavi-

She looked from the still-hot tool in Zulavi's grip, to her unprotected leg - her breath catching on the fumes. *He'd branded her! A brief glimpse of the part-cauterised, part-wet wound across her thigh showed her too much and assured her of much more.*

Her world wanted to spin again but she conquered the feeling as understanding pooled, further drenching her. *He'd deliberately branded her to cut past the walls protecting her Soul Reach; to bring her back to face consequence! It hadn't shattered her Link with the more basic State of Veranto, but it surely didn't matter now...*

Stomach clenching, her body reacted before her mind could caution, a sudden descend of terror sending her into a fit of panic. The chains that shackled her to the rack rattled. *He'd branded her! He'd taken that flecking hot metal to her leg, and-*

Through the whine of chains and the pointless straining against bonds she'd never break, she heard Simarovien Zulavi laugh as if amused by her loss of control and for a moment her anger wiped away all that would undo her, rolling it under a blanket of descending calm that had little origins in Veranto and everything to do with her own ruddy failure to improve her disposition - or better yet: to have avoided this dungeon altogether!

It killed her struggles. The realisation of what he'd do unhinged her but she felt no pain, and with the clarity of poorly-embraced acceptance, she knew it truly didn't matter now; that it was indeed just a matter of time now. *A matter of time before everything was lost...*

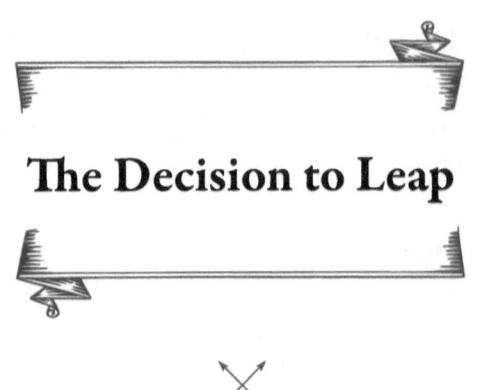

The Decision to Leap

A SQUALL OF EVERYTHING uncertain and detrimental seemed to linger in the wake of both thoughts and words. Malandar was uncomfortably aware that much hinged on the Elvern King's willingness to release Thessilia. *Bizarrely, it struck him that it was an awareness of a calibre similar to that of the afterglow in one's soul after being ravished by a stronger Weaver's magic. The event would pass - but the recollection... the invasion... the surrender...*

Uncommonly uncomfortable, he couldn't smother the sensation and it made him think again of the 'restraints'; of how he should be explaining certain aspects to Thessilia now; of how he ought to tell her about 'the plan' now that he intended to stray from the path of collecting the Tarvia in favour of searching out the Sentient Magic.

But she'd oppose him, and he was tired, and it was – *for now* - somehow very convenient to let her stay submerged in the belief that he'd somehow managed to track down some of the old artefacts. It was a feasible scenario, not to mention the conclusion he knew she'd already made when he'd told her what to relay to the Speaker. *Did it not make sense to spare himself sufferance for a while longer?*

But he'd be dealing with Sentient True Magic and the fact that he felt an obligation to alert his fellow Guardians was becoming an in-dismissible weight upon the wrong side of the balance between caution versus reason. The pull of this magic was like an icy string of pure, unpolluted power connecting straight to his heart and mind, *unharvested*, a source to provoke desire and inspire the impossible, but it was also without law unless curbed and bound. How would he – or any other Guardian - manage to slip out of their long-standing belief that one should not simply destroy it once located? He did not have the cohort of a Tower behind him; did not intend to apply 'the Elvern way' either, though he was also aware that maybe he'd never get a choice. Was he deluded in thinking he might successfully break procedure to try and untangle this unstable element of magic, even for the gain of the Upper Circle? Indeed, was there not a very good reason why most realms had called upon their best Talent to carry out the best singular solution when it came to neutralising these Neidar Ba'raie; when it came to protecting everyone and everything from these abhorrent fonts of eroding unpredictable power?

Malandar knew it could be done differently, however; just as he knew himself usually infallible and thereby perfectly capable of doing what he planned regardless of valid concerns aroused by the Speaker, or more to the crux, some prissy self-questioning part of himself. Like it or not, he was of Elvern descend and the Elvern had done this thing repeatedly, stretching over the aeons and to good – if morally questionable - effect. Sure, without the traditional 'aides', it was reportedly much like carrying a scoop of dragons' tears in a bowl made of decaying wood whilst hoping that the chemical make-up of this concoction would stay balanced for long enough to get you to the area of proper containment - but it could be done. Providing he was in time...

Of course, ethically speaking, the Elvern process was wrong on so many levels he deliberately refrained from thinking about it, but certainly, in the face of what they were up against, Malandar feared that none of them could afford to hold on to their refined ideas much longer. The spirit of Marlan within him was not the haunting of a person wronged in death, but a reflection of Malandar's own issues; a reflection of morally decaying questions that might once have needed to remain protected as guarded truth, yet could now no longer be defended under that same premise of justification. *'What will you do? Risk it? Don't risk it?' Once again the path had only one outcome... yet this time, there was still leeway to manoeuvre, and this time...*

Yet all the same, he could hear Thessilia argue that he wasn't exactly what you'd call 'defenceless'; that he had the Power of the Circle behind him; that he still carried the knowledge and the experience to win this fight without plucking at extremes; that the Maker would right the magic! And on every point, she should've been right. Except that he already knew that she'd be wrong, which made this doubly difficult, particularly when it came to the Speakers sensitive persuasions.

'*So the Speaker has met somebody, you were saying?*' he ventured abruptly, completing the final check of the horses, head-sore with his own lack of faith and the continuous streak of troublesome insight.

'*He has.*' Guardian Emara confirmed just as he slung the hated saddle across Well's back with an inward wince for the need to subject himself to the 'torture' so soon after stopping.

Oblivious, Thessilia continued, '*Yes apparently it is someone of Talent it would seem and the Maker knows this must be so; the Speaker does not usually take an interest in anyone, and yet he does now?*'

Malandar heard the other Guardian's slight question, married up with a slash of what seemed just a sliver of fondness and goodwill: Thessilia clearly indulging herself to embrace a touch of personal merriment at this unusual turn. Continuing, she elaborated, '*But evidently this one is different: a child; a Seer. She might show us the path, he tells me; she might read us the past – and the future. And so, he has taken her as his apprentice.*'

With a surge of surprise Malandar straightened from cinching the saddle girth, the task momentarily forgotten.

'*Good Maker, how unusual!*' he exclaimed, weighing the impact of such a turn, almost with a smile of his own for this unprecedented development. *So... seemed he was not the only one with a personal agenda. How liberating.*

'*Guess I should have known our Speaker had a valid reason to trail back to the Sabén-Heshep,*' he mused, taken with the idea that the Speaker had appropriated a tiny witch into his services, thereby supplying a levy. '*But why did he not speak of this on the day of the Quickening? It would have made good sense to alert the Circle.*'

'*Sense? Would it?*' Thessilia questioned, piqued. '*Commander Denarlin, we're ever a secretive bunch, are we not? Don't we ever always hold something back from the others? In this instance we're talking about a child. An Elvern Child, sure, but a child nonetheless. Would you have approved? Would any of us? Surely all that counts is that he has moved to aid the common goal? Is that not our purpose, providing we move within the Laws?*'

Thessilia painted an unfortunate truth and Malandar nearly grimaced at the irony and offered her a mental nod of concord. '*Well since we do not com-*

monly involve children in our actions to stay the Mad Ones, then no, I guess I would not have approved. However, if the Speaker has a compelling reason, then I can hardly stand in argument. Times are... different.'

Ignoring Thessilia's edgy surprise at his comment, Malandar returned himself to the task at hand, went to the bay's headgear, and buckled up the loosened straps. *'And this girl... this Seer? She is strong enough to do this?'*

'She is Sheshem'Kufunar's daughter. She has had the gift since birth and if she did not know of us before, I strongly suspect she'll be quite aware now. I get the feeling that she is on the cusp of womanhood, at which point there will be little hiding from her anyway. I'd say she is well within the grounds of 'capable', and I certainly doubt she'll be scarred by the knowledge she gathers! Apparently, she possesses a rogue talent that does not quite follow the Tapestry as well, and I believe they consider her guilty of lies. Needless to say, the Speaker thinks otherwise and as she is not in favour with the Council nor with the Chief of Vectors, the Speaker has taken charge - as a favour to the Watchéran, though one might argue whose favouring who here?

'In any event, if the girl is innocent of the real world, he will protect her and with a youngster like that, who knows, maybe the little one might even manage to wheedle her way into Guardian Mehand'Arun's affections? Unlikely I know, but still... wouldn't that be a pip?'

'Oh a pip indeed,' Malandar agreed dryly.

In reality, he suspected they'd be far more likely to witness a Blight Rider plant flowers than they ever would be of knowing a day when Rhindarhlar Mehand'Arun would be showing a girl of the Sabén-Heshep any warmth, but he kept the sentiment to himself. *'And does this miracle-girl have a name that we might know her by?'*

'He calls her Nefer... Nefer'Kemnebit. She did not give him her name. She was introduced, as is proper. Apparently, he Weaved her a live Sunerai miniature-panther for a present; a name-sake it would seem. He told me 'her eyes nearly popped'. Popped! Can you believe that was the exact term he used?'

Bemused, Malandar slowed his work with the horses once more and cocked an eyebrow at the twilight. *'The Speaker did what?'*

At his incredulity, the other Guardian smiled and he felt her mood turning softly-affable to have raised in him a touch of rare sentiment. *'Yes indeed! It's a pip! The old man is getting soft.'*

This time he did smile. A soft twitch at the corners of his mouth – a change seen only by the emerging stars above. *Her reflection of delight was endearing. However much Thessilia might have disagreed with the Speaker in the first hours after their Quickening, she did not hold a grudge now and it was heartening; as usual, she understood the stakes and did not shy from duty.* His brief smile soon fading, however - his eyes taking on a distant edge of those very stars above - Malandar drew a rasping breath.

He really should confide in her...

'You asked to know my plans.' he stated briskly as he tied the two other horses' lead ropes to the saddle with a snap of leather as if to punctuate his decision and waylay all reservations for long enough to carry on.

Emara stirred like a predator, shattering all sentiments of endearment, but he barely noticed. Once the words were spoken, he could not retract them, and on her part, Thessilia Emara needn't confirm; the push against his mind as she directed all her attentive inquisitiveness towards him was enough to assure him that she would not back down now, so there...

'It is my intention to trap a Neidar Ba'raie.' he informed her then, now without a quiver of regret, feeling calm detachment return to him in the very moment the thought had been communicated - and rightly so. The Speaker had called himself a young apprentice into the equation, Thessilia was going to leave the Elvern to patrol their own realm; there was a time he'd never have approved the idea of using children in furthering the Upper Circle's cause, but now?

As First Guardian, he was justified to set this plan in motion... *discounting all the possible consequences he might unleash, of course!*

'Hmm,' Guardian Emara grunted, her mind a stream of calm against his; not at all what he'd been expecting. *'Bold idea, I'd say; didn't know any existed. Still... a Neidar Ba'raie is dangerous though; Sentient True Magic is... is volatile.'* She paused, feelings momentarily voiding from the link; caution riding care, she hesitated for a beat, then asked the one question, he'd known must come.

'Commander, are you certain this is a wise decision?'

'Certain?' Malandar quipped, though his tone turned stark. *'No Guardian, I am certain of very little these days, but it is the only avenue that makes sense - providing we want to thwart the Mad Ones! After everything we've been dealt, we all know it will take something... something 'different'. Something... 'Unexpected'.*

Now if I curb the Neidar Ba'raie and seal the Power to my name, it could turn the odds.'

'Hmmm yes, this is true... providing you are in time, First Guardian!' With her usual ability to hit the heart of a topic centre-on, Thessilia let the statement hang, then finished, *'And if you are not?'*

'If I am not,' he carried on, taking up her line, *'then I will do the necessary as a kindness before the Venzoians can put in a Harvest - but I feel the draw of untarnished power. I must be in time. Anything else is inconceivable!'*

'Yes I suppose it is,' she allowed without argument, *'But pray tell, Commander Denarlin, how do you plan to do this? And what would you have me tell the Speaker? Even with the use of Aquedian Wards, this is not a path I'd commend, not even for a Guardian; and the Laws of Existence do not allow us-*

'I mean: the Speaker, he will—'

'Malandar interrupted, *'The Speaker may keep his opinions or share them with the Circle as he pleases. Indeed, he can spirit-walk to petition the Maker for council if he feels conflicted but he should remember that this is my responsibility, just as that Seer is his. Now this is my Word as Guardian Commander and as such, beyond contestation. I suppose you'll tell him that.'*

Thessilia fell deadly quiet. *'Aha, so it's like that...'*

'Change has backed us into a corner; it has already crippled us - and it's about to hit again! In more ways than one! Thessilia, old friend, you are right, of course: this should not be commended and I pray by the Power of my Word and the Light in my Core that I will be able to pull this off! However, if I don't...'

'I know, Malandar.' Thessilia injected with a sigh. She'd suspended with formality now, he expected, only because he'd also allowed it to slip, and because - between the two of them - there was something in this debate that reeked of old times before the Maker.

'And you can do it,' she told him suddenly with a smile to belie the severity of her persistent frown.

The same warmth he'd known from her before the Upper Circle, filtered down their connection like a glimmer of sunlight as she continued with conviction, *'Yes... if anyone could ever do such a mad thing, it'd be you. It's buried in your ancestry. And it'll come like second nature, I expect – though without the use of Aquedian Wards, you'll have to be exceptionally 'charming', of course.'*

'But of course,' he echoed, lips twitching at the idea of how well she still knew him.

Touching a nerve in them both, she mixed acute banter with curious serenity, *'Oh, how I fear Richarmarlan would've been proud of you for this. Very proud! However, personal persuasions aside, in my humble view, a few Aquedian Wards might still prove helpful in this, though...'*

'I don't intend to apply that barbaric skill in my approach!' he refuted, left foot hitting the stirrup to hoist himself smoothly into the saddle-of-horror. *'There are other ways of affecting an agreeable outcome and I will not miss the lack of vile Elvern magic to pollute my intentions!'*

For a moment Thessilia enveloped him with nothing but pure agreement and Malandar gifted her with a genuine, rare smile down the bond.

'Now if I have to be charming, so be it-' he grinned with a thought to the past, though what mirth he showed her soon faded to seriousness, *'-but, I seriously doubt it will be that easy! After all... with a Neidar Ba'raie, it never is!'*

Thessilia offered Malandar a nod... *sanctioning?*

'And truer words may never have been perceived,' she breathed, quietly, even as the First Guardian nudged the bay into a slow trot that drew the other two horses into single file behind him.

'Intriviatu al hastriviatu, Commander Denarlin. You will keep us posted... I hope.'

And before the First Guardian might offer the appropriate reply, Guardian Emara retracted the sensitive link beyond hope of recall.

He exhaled. *There... the first imaginary ledge lay behind him. Hopefully he could float on the trade winds for a while: hopefully for long enough to make the inevitable crash worth it.*

Malandar smiled to himself with a slash of acerbic humour. His uncle would probably not appreciate the jest, but at least Malandaar'Vahran Denarlin found that latter thought rather worthy of the irony behind it.

Now, as for what the Maker would say or do, he could not imagine, but the Laws remained clear. *He was still First Guardian. A Neidar Ba'raie was still a Neidar Ba'raie. And this would hurt.*

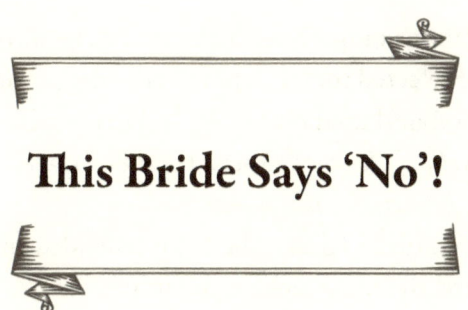

This Bride Says 'No'!

Solancei found Zulavi with her eyes.

For a wonder, he had the grace not to gloat. Actually, for a wonder, his face revealed very little emotion past the subdued infestation of trouble that blighted his triumph but betrayed him to his surroundings only by the lines that cut his brow and the slight upward tilt of his chin.

Relinquishing a pent back exhale, he relaxed though she hadn't been aware he was tensing. Waving for Swentor and allowing the older man to relieve him of the plain torture instrument he settled one hip casually against the edge of the rack whilst he shot her a flat assessing stare that captivated his sore state of mind perfectly. *He must have more questions now...*

Solancei rolled her eyes away. The rustle of coal was too loud as the minion Swentor poked the rod back into the deep basin, raising a rush of heat. It spiked a tendril of apprehension but she could not cope with Zulavi seeing such weakness and besides... the idea of the promised Meer'ron was instantly there to distract her from other, simpler horrors. *Mercy, if they drugged her with that poison now...*

"Good Gods, grey-eyes - that pesky trick of yours...!" Zulavi's choice tone caught her in its web of unwanted but perplexing intrigue, and though she hadn't intended to do so, Solancei returned her gaze to his.

Pursing his lips, accompanying the move with the merest kink of his head, he allowed her the grace of a mild salute, saying, "I guess you did not exaggerate then when you declared that the Meer'ron would be of no effect. Poor Swentor here could not even get it down you, but fleck grey-eyes... I trust you understand that when you then slowed your breathing, I felt compelled to do something."

As if she could fail to comprehend his meaning, he waved a hand briefly to-wards the handful of selected tools steeping in the fire pit next to the smoulder-ing length of flat metal he'd used on her leg and her insides curdled. *She under-stood him perfectly well; understood exactly what he'd done; what he was saying - but what cut was not his actions, it was hers...*

He'd broken her Link to Klaas - she comprehended his fault in this – but the failure, the wasted time, the lacking discipline... *that... that was all on her!* For a fact she'd probably never learn if there'd been a correlation between his interfering and the strain it had been to open - and maintain - the Moment Out of Time in the manner that the Scroll had instructed. Yet for sure, whether by clever design or simple luck, Simarovien Zulavi's drastic action had certainly in-terrupted at the worst opportune time and by then she'd have nothing more to give, nothing left with which to fight or to stand against it. He'd branded her with that rod! *To wrench her back to this world, he'd branded her like a common piece of livestock. And, with as little regard!*

That she had trouble wrapping her mind around everything that had hap-pened, didn't matter. In every sense, her cards were all played, and... and Iambre...

Mercy, but Iambre would pay the price of her Shield's failure, just as... *just as she'd always dreaded!*

Hollow fear for the future well-being of her friend curbed Solancei's self-disgust, numbing her against the thoughts that she knew must come next. The Soul Reach had not burned out her skill, but Zulavi would not relent. The Ve-ranto Link would fail and the severance would be painful and treacherous even without Meer'ron poisoning, and then-

She stared at the Knights Commander for one moment longer, her mind ailing to accept defeat. Part of her wanted dearly to lift her head and survey the damage to her leg and yet she had no will; no need. *It would be bad. Like every-thing else about the cursed situation, it would be bad – Zulavi did nothing half measure! Had she not been wrapped in the State of Veranto, the act of mutilation would have hurt deep enough to unhinge the mind, but at least she'd been spared that! As for what lay next though-*

Her thoughts refused to finish that sentence, for it would finish her.

Sudden nausea rising, she retched again. Burns could heal but she no longer thought she'd be around for long enough to care, should the wound become weepy and sceptic. *She would give Zulavi what he wanted: she'd give him the answers to pursue his zealous vendetta on the Enclave, and she would betray Iambre too: provide him with enough leverage to aid his plans a hundredfold. Time... this was simply about time.*

Solancei sucked in air and closed her eyes.

She was drained; so, so tired... and the irony of her predicament cut her so closely that for a moment she came ridiculously close to laughing out loud. *Gods, but this was insane... she was done for, but there would be no rest for her. Not for a very long, haunting while...*

Feeling drunk on her own exhaustion, she drew a shuddering breath. *Iambre... forgive me. Forgive...*

"So I sent the good Swentor off for another pitcher of Meer'ron, by the way."

Zulavi injected the words casually, the incidental slant somehow cruelly pitched but assuring her that this respite would be just as brief as imagined. Ignoring him because it was all the power she had to influence the situation, Solancei refused to acknowledge the words, however, and she soon she heard him turn away.

His absence brought mild relief. Yet from the sound and direction of his steps, she could tell he'd crossed to the fire - a fact the subsequent rustle of someone vigorously stroking up the coals confirmed would be to her disadvantage. She clenched her fists, ignoring Mitail and his weighing, clammy eyes.

She hadn't felt that iron bite her leg before, but the very idea of anyone lowering that instrument to her skin seemed to liquefy her bones, yet still worse than that, was Zulavi's reference to Swentor. The crony would fetch more Meer'ron; she could not fight that and she could not believe her own lies to the opposite because eventually, they'd successfully administer the poison!

Absurdly, it occurred to her for the first time that this was what people would call 'torture' and her innards churned at the idea, purging some of the lethargic fatigue. In its place, a shot of new energy flashed through her like a drug in itself: infusing her with a throbbing sense of nervous readiness that was a purely natural response utterly separate from the Veranto – and thereby, useless. However, it found her briefly 'face-to-face' once more with the freezing cold that seemed to linger in her core like a slowly shifting glazier, expanding and contracting as though alive; as though it would like nothing better than for her to stretch out a mental hand and claim it.

For shame, she would have done now. Had she possessed the strength, she would have reached for the oblivion it promised, but not even the new-found beguiling starlight in her core was enough to arouse her for more than a breath or two. Holding even this basic link with the Veranto was becoming a strain but this was where she chose to spend her strength; she latched on, giving herself no quarter and revelling in the feel of it: *enjoying the final embrace for a few last moments before-*

"So what exactly did you manage to tell them, I wonder?" Zulavi questioned, not pensive but demanding, and for a split heartbeat Solancei did not know to what he referred. Then the unmistakable creek of the cell door interrupted.

Solancei went cold. It could only mean that Swentor had returned!

Twisting her neck with an effort rooted in desperate longing to see anyone but the crony, she felt her mouth go as dry as good kindling when her hopes were dashed. Swentor was steadying a pale slender stone jar between two gloved hands, a single stout cup assigned to the crook of one elbow, as he came forward with a keen look in the eye and the sheen of nervous anticipation glistening across the brow.

Their eyes met. Solancei felt rend in stone as he smirked like a backyard bully and her gaze shot to the jar.

Harvested Megaa'ron seeds could be smoked, chewed, ingested, burned, all in a dozen repulsive ways - but like many poisons, drying reduced potency whilst steeping to produce the Meer'ron poison, served to revive, sometimes even heighten, the effects. *Whatever the contents of that jug, she feared it would cripple her! Even were it not a heavy dose, she knew enough about it to speculate on how it would assuredly send her mind and awareness adrift and that this in turn would sever her concentration, then cut her Link with the Veranto! It would happen as surely as these shackles bound her, and after-*

"You know what I bring you, don't you?" Looking directly at her with an eerie smoulder in the eye, Swentor offered her a soft smile, guaranteeing how his thoughts must match her own as he rounded the rack to most dutifully take up a position of patience by her feet.

She swallowed hard.

The origins of the subtle sweetness on her tongue no longer in question, she imagined she ought to also keep an eye on Zulavi, yet couldn't seem to help her mind comply. *There was no moisture in her mouth and her throat contracted painfully...*

The desiccated rustle of coal being stirred and prodded sounded like the mocking laughter of ancient animated corpses as the sustained manipulation cranked up the temperature emitted from the centrally sunken pit. In the intensifying glow, the rock looked dull and sullen: the layers of soot, generated from smoke and poor ventilation, clearly absorbing the firelight and smothering hope.

To escape the cluster of thoughts in her head, Solancei turned her attention towards Zulavi finally. She was faced only with his back but Mitail's eyes fell on her, then spirited sideways towards Zulavi with a smirk. She knew the older crony was scared of her and suspected he hated her for inciting such weakness. She also knew he hated how she'd crippled his fellow Regulators-in-Arms; hated how she'd reacted to his foul touch, spurning his sleek promises in return for vile favours, and he certainly hated how she'd bit him; hated how he been forced to use her pendant to secure new peace between himself and his master - and there was probably more. That man had his own daggers to bury; indeed, she hardly needed eyes to see the extent to which he was enjoying her awareness as every moment drew her closer to the final score.

Refusing to acknowledge the bastard's imminent triumph; refusing to hear or see what Zulavi was doing, Solancei shifted her eyes to the fissures above. Every sound, every breath was like soft torture on her imagination. The air was shimmering with heat. *What were they waiting for?*

The silence widened. Solancei had the sudden unpleasant cut of insight that the Knights Commander was about to drag something extra into this fray. But what? Realising that he'd ceased his manipulation of the heated instruments, she felt him sidestep to turn his back on the fire. Her heart thumped.

"Well I realise you will not talk of course,-" Aware of the subtle shift of shadows as Zulavi moved, Solancei felt him turn his cool, weighing regard in her direction once more, "-but still it barely matters, grey-eyes. I will know everything soon enough, including what exactly you managed to share with your circle of Masters and then we'll make plans to counter, so really... this has just been an unnecessary dance around the inevitable after all."

In spite better judgement, Solancei looked towards him. For a blink it seemed that darkness was hemming her in, then her sight corrected itself just as he expelled a deep breath with an edge of nuisance that she imagined might be linked to her lacking reaction. It was incidental. She would have loved to call it rebellious bravery, but in actual fact, she was just too spent - and the outward signs of weaning emotional investment simply a product of her fatigue. The State of Veranto was little more than a hazy bubble in her mind; there was no longer enough strength to pull herself into the Link in the way that would support distance and serenity, but still... how was he to know?

"What has been set in motion cannot be so easily stopped, you know,-" he commented in terse tones, "-but that trick of yours...! My grey-eyes, I will salute your utterly brilliant stroke of strategy - and felicitations indeed, for now I just don't know what your acquaintance will cost me - and *that* insecurity leaves me vexed in a manner you could not even begin to comprehend!'"

Solancei rolled her gaze from his. *Deliberately dismissing.* It wasn't hard. She was finding it a challenge to concentrate on his words. Her vision dimmed, then realigned. In a belayed slash of insight, she realised he was angry. *Very angry, and all because-.*

She snapped for breath, a curious sense of incredulity spreading within her. *Mercy, so he did not know that he'd successfully foiled her Soul Reach; he had no clue that she had failed to call attention to his treachery...*

The coals rustled again, the sound as desiccated as Zulari'Chi's laughter across the Void. She heard Zulavi move. She would have preferred to face the God and not the man right then, but something odd still swelled within. *He did not know...*

"So you realise of course that we are at a crossroad's here." Like a magnet Zulavi drew her gaze to him, using a semi-reasonable lilt that masked the anger she'd sensed only moments earlier. He was poking at the fire again as if he was stabbing his own nuisance and newly-hatched grief deep into the burning coals but then he turned to offer her prone form a coldly contemplating look over one shoulder. It chilled the ice in her core several degrees and a spike of odd fear shot down her spine. His glacial eyes held the reflections of horrors and dreams in their depths: something she would have paid dearly never to have seen...

Slowly, he drew one of the blade-like instruments from the hot embers, adjusting his handhold slightly as the smouldering tool inched clear.

The elaborate precision of the action sent a wave of sick fascination through her core. He was wearing a padded leather glove on his right hand, and from the way he handled the red-golden length of metal, she was assured he possessed practice beyond that which had been done to her leg already.

The wave of sickness became a river tinged by fear that seemed to thin her blood. The tool looked like an unfinished short-sword that had been beaten into rough shape but still needed the attention of a good blacksmith to complete the process from raw resource to weapon. *She could not imagine anyone callous enough to touch it to another person's skin - but her ailing imagination of the man's level of cruelty didn't matter, of course; the lack of finish on the would-be blade didn't matter; she knew he did not intend to run her through with it...*

Live dread twisted within her, stealing what was left of courage. Like before, when she'd seen the jug of Meer'ron in Swentor's hands, she now just couldn't seem to take her eyes off Zulavi either, as he – *as though to contemplate the suitability of the white-glowing metal* - paused leisurely to survey his tool of choice.

It was like watching an artist select the right shade of paint before going to work on a new canvas and fear seemed to cut deep rivulets into her then, rushing now like a raging icy river into her core to sweep away everything but some base sliver of instinct that would have sent her bolting under more favourable circumstances.

Solancei didn't know how she managed to hold onto the State of Veranto then: she couldn't seem to breathe. His calculating eyes swung from the metal to hers - and her heart thumped once in hard pain as it stumbled several times over its supposed own beat.

Then Simarovien Zulavi started towards the rack, *towards her,* the length of the crude blade carefully angled up and away so as not to accidentally touch anything. *Mercy...*

A lance of blind angst sawed through Solancei.

From Zulavi's tight face she read that his intentions were as hot as the golden-white edges of the instrument he carried and she did not want him any closer now, not after what he'd already done with that other brand. *The iron looked hot enough to cauterise – no hotter!*

Panic snapping its teeth at her jocular, Solancei push herself sideways what minuscule inches allowed her. Her breaths had become an erratic chant in her own ears: brief and hard, but not fulfilling; not... *not sustaining.*

Fuelled by despair she twisted her chin to see if she'd somehow missed a trick with the cuffs; to see if she could somehow-

It was not going to work, of course, rationally she already knew this: the jab of despair welled up like black tar to taunt her nativity as it tainted her last fringe of control. *This was not a bluff! He'd use that instrument and never blink...*

"So, here's the thing,-" he began, giving her a strange look, "-the way I view it, in reality Anchan'Chi may be a Bride short or not, but how will I ever know? Verily, your words are manifold and you raise beguiling possibilities of the truth with the mere twist of your splendid mind, but perhaps it matters not. See, I rather think that your extensive talents did honour Him, and yet here I am, about to steal them one and all; it might not please him!"

Zulavi paused as though to gauge her reaction. *In his hand, the hot metal seemed to pulse...*

Solancei clenched her teeth, straining her jaw. She didn't know the meaning of his cryptic remarks but her well-developed sense of danger recognised the trap long-shut behind her back then and the icy river within seemed to rush down the length of her body in a way that very nearly rendered void what little dignity she still possessed...

With a dismissive smirk, he overlooked her discomfort.

"So I once saw them make two Brides for Him you know," Zulavi informed, upper lip curling slightly as a symbol of his aversion as he took another step closer, "I assure you it was undeniably unsavoury business if one is squeamish, and yet...

"Well quite oddly, I recall thinking that there was a certain poetry to the act as well. See grey-eyes, I recall thinking that branding of his mark on the shoulder is one thing, but that the ritual scarring of a new Bride is truly something... something that puts leagues between a simple soldier seeking affiliation and a fine elite of first-class Brides."

Zulavi glanced at his tool and shook his head as if in silent admiration of some unknown woman's pluck. In musing tones, he ventured, "To be a Bride: to declare oneself ready to give everything that He demands and then offer more as a mark of respect...?

"I'd call it perfection, grey-eyes. *Perfection.* However, were you aware that He does not accept them all? Did you know that He will spurn the offering if the Bride does not... does not manage to win his unending favour? It seems almost sad that someone could fail such a test, but then again, it takes hours to turn the flesh and spirit of a warrior into an unyielding tool. *Hours!* Only the strongest survive. And then... as for the taking of an eye!"

Solancei shivered. His musings held her riveted in an ugly place between revulsion and twisted fascination. There was a reason for his strange monologue – there had to be – but she didn't want to find out. Zulavi smiled: a raptor's grimace.

"Incidentally, did anyone ever tell you how the latter detail is to do with the Bride forever keeping one eye on the fight and the other eye on no other man but He-who-is-her-Master? I confess I believed it hearsay, but it's in the scripture and I find it an interesting concept: to belong so utterly to a deity that your very existence is theirs to command? To have that belonging, it... it must be intoxicating!"

Solancei blinked. "Sure. Undoubtedly."

Upon hearing her terse infliction, Zulavi paused as if surprised. "No? No, you don't think so, I suppose. But why, grey-eyes? I think you could do it – after all, you need a place to belong, don't you? A worthy master whom you might serve with indiscriminate love and loyalty. A master beyond the Enclave and their false ideals: nothing wasted! All in Balance! And why not rectify the situation, grey-eyes? Being what I am – and who I am, why not kill two snakes with one arrow and both get your secrets *and* appease our glorious Lord of War by offering him a fine token?"

"Rectify the situation? Token?" she mumbled, new tiny slashes of fear tiptoeing with razor claws along her senses as the undercurrent of his words began to untwist, straightening her perception and finally aligning her understanding with his. Like someone had stabbed her in the guts, she lost all care for everything else other than the next breath as cold, terrible terror drenched her in sweat. *He could not-*

"No... no! No, you cannot do that!" she spluttered, eyes growing wide as the impact of his threat penetrated deeper and deeper.

Ignoring her, Simarovien tilted his chin. He looked to be appraising her. *Like a nag destined for the terrines might be assessed for the potential value and volume of meat.*

Desperation claiming her, she stuttered, "You... you cannot... you should not... you... you are not ordained... this is not a temple... I... NO!"

"Ah but grey-eyes, embrace your fortune," he invited in a most reasonable voice, "We needn't be in a temple for this to be considered a sacred act. All of Castle Zanzier is a dedicated shrine to His will and honour: we are on holy ground, I am His most devout acolyte, and you a most worthy gift irrespective of your possible prior affiliations, so why not curry favour towards the success of my future endeavours? It's just good business – oh and perhaps a bit of pay-back too."

"No!" Solancei knew she'd paled under the dirt, but she could not force her voice above a shaky whisper as his true intentions left her reeling. "No! No, I will not consent to this! I will not be made a Bride! You cannot! I refuse!"

"Oh grey-eyes, your voice is sweeter than oil rubbed on sore muscles,-" he looked pleased, a genuine expression which made her hairs stand on end, "-but you should worry not. If you should falter; if our gracious God does not want you, rest assured that my men still will! You will lack for neither purpose nor want for company, and you shall have enough poison to drown your happiness or sorrows just like any other spurned servant of the Parthenon, so am I not merciful on this day; am I not forgiving after your show of disobedience in front of all of Zanzier's worst?"

Solancei bit her bottom lip to stop it from quivering. *The man was mad! Utterly, utterly mad. And she was trapped.*

Zulavi lifted the roughly-profiled, glowing blade. "I know this goes against the common order of things, but what say you we begin then with... say... an eye?"

Swallowing a Bitter Draught

SOLANCEI'S BREATH HITCH as strains terror compressed her chest - for a moment constricting everything except her imagination. *An eye? An eye?!*

Her voice rose in consternation, "You're mad. This is madness!"

Her fear must have leaked into her expression, for Zulavi bent forward a little - offering her an almost cheerful smile, but it was a smile rooted in some acid-drenched notion of enmity, and... *and something more... something that reeked of him dancing the line between religious avarice and strange exhilaration.*

Of course, he wouldn't care to hear her stupid pleas and yet she thought she heard herself repeat, "No... no this is not right! Please, you cannot do this!"

A bead of moisture sauntered down her neck. Twisting uselessly to add whatever hairs breaths she might between herself and the heat emitted from the length of iron as it began to dip, Solancei already knew she was going to beg harder.

"No,-" she tried again, her voice a rasp of panic, but Mitail seemed to swoop into her line of sight out of nowhere, effortlessly looping a length of knotted cord around her forehead. Without pause, he yanked the spare tight, effectively shattering her plea into a wordless grunt as he pulled her face towards him at an angle that lost her sight of Zulavi.

"No please," she gasped again, heartbeat exploding, "Please, we can-"

Mitail struck her. Not hard like the last time, but his action enough to break the intended outburst. In a blink, anger spiked within her: a stab of a dagger that burst from her core like a cornered beast provoked to make a final sally to save itself from hunters.

Yanking hard to rid herself of his interference, the cord sawed into her skull, earning her a burst of unexpected pain along her temple. It saw another fear return. *The fear of losing the Link, or worse...*

She tried to breathe; to assure herself that she could hold on, and the pain subsided. It left her weak; new words, new requests of mercy, got stuck in her throat. *Her head remained immobilised, the entire right side of her face throbbing where it was buried hard against the inner surface of her upper right arm, whilst the left side was rendered exposed...*

She had little control now, splinters of dread savaged her insides – an electrifying feeling that made her pant and struggle doubly hard whilst the starlight became a jarring pulse of slashing razors. For a moment Mitail was so close that she could hear his rushed breath; could smell his excitement - then her own beating heart seemed to drown out the sound as the crony stepped free and Zulavi stepped close. She did not want to look but she could not dismiss what she saw from the corner of her eye either. It did not help that the tool had lost a little of its glow: it had not yet cooled enough not to work as he intended, for the metal remained a vibrant smouldering orange.

Residual heat made her eyes water and her skin flush. Sudden sweat stung her cut lip; drenched her hair. *The Knights Commander was lowering the rod...*

"No, please! You can't!" This time she pushed the words forth, her voice breaking on the plea. With a debilitating mixture of disbelief and piercing dread, she struggled against the cord and felt it dig into her forehead in such a way that the pressure couldn't even be masked by the shreds of Veranto she still clung to.

"No, no don't!" her voice became a guttural yelp as Mitail yanked her face further right, twisting her neck into an uncomfortable angle that threatened to pop her upper vertebrae out of alignment. She had a blink to wish that they would all be swallowed by the Void; a blink to feel as cornered as a trapped animal: as furious with wrath and panic, for she wanted to rip out her own limbs and latch on to their throats to protect herself and mete out vengeance in spades for what had been done; for what was being done, and-

Sometimes 'forever' lived in a few heartbeats: a flash of Zulavi's still-pristine coat, a feeling of intense glowing heat so full on that it seemed to set her entire face alight - then the fire-heated instrument dipped the final inch and bit deep, hissing like a tangle of snakes...

She felt body jerk just once, the part-searing of her skin like an instant sun-burn that singed an exposed eyebrow and burned away wisps of loose hair to the roots. *She heard men breathing too loudly. Jarring sensitive ears, the iron touch seemed to hiss forever. She felt nothing, but the heat was unbearable...*

Something twanged, releasing her head from its awkward position, but she could see nothing through the rising plume of smoke, could sense even less, and then she was choking on the caustic stench of flesh on fire!

At the same time, a myriad of tiny impressions pressed against her aware-ness. *For a moment she did not know if she was hallucinating again? If this was still part of her attempt to effect a Soul Reach?*

In her mind's eye, she saw the flash of fire ignite near her face, acrid smoke following to a blazing cacophony of sound that seemed to saturate the air with a raw swishing fizzle. Somehow interlaced with the dream-like sound, some-body's hard, weeping breaths of heightened fright seemed enhanced by the bruising pull she exacted on the bounds that held her immobilised. Something touched her left cheek – feather light and fast: a series of rapid scores and then fresh blood flowed, at once both ice and fire...

A fine thread of pain made a muscle in her jaw jump. The too-cool air seemed to scorch her like a lover's silken caress where the iron had stolen away layers of ruined skin, exposing bone and sinew. The air stank. Within her the Veranto wavered but held, sparing her from bodily pain, though not under-standing. Then a strange notion of self and place stole through her, hotly pur-sued by a wave of detachment. *Detachment... so much detachment. Then... noth-ing.*

Not realising how she'd held her breath, Solancei gasped, choking on lin-gering smoke and shock yet again and for a moment she was not the only one as she awoke to the sound of Mitail's hacking coughs grating in her ears. In the State of Veranto, the complete lack of pain made the vandalism of her face hard to relate to: the smells of the bowel-turning, noxious fumes it had wrought seemed somehow harder to accept although the scent of burned hair mingled with the reek of charred flesh and salty blood on every breath she gasped down. The men shifted in and out of focus around her; the cell seemed to dance-

She felt surreal. This was not real; it couldn't be...

Somewhere Swentor's coughs echoed twice to mingle with the other crony's and her mind remained strangely void as darkness and light warred; she couldn't see properly...

For a moment she floated in a peculiar vacuum; time was measured by the intermittent but free flow of blood as it crawled from the cuts on her cheek, across her chin and down her neck. It seemed too regular a feeling and for moments she almost slipped away, then a flash of her former panic reasserted itself, burrowing deep like larvae of Coover River Flies.

A startling sensation, she twisted her head sharply. Strange feelings re-enacting something akin to discomfort when she realised that unless she shifted accordingly, she couldn't see anything to her left side. *Nothing at all.*

A thin whimper of distress escaped her. Her nostrils flared as she sought to contain the queer feeling that writhed deep within: shock pushing to the fore. *The stench was horrendous but denial made her bold: her vision would be fine. Her perception was marred but she'd be right!*

Still, as revulsion stretched her thinner with every breath, a strange tingling sensation began to emanate from the newly created injury, belying her pallid self-assurance. Soon the familiar soft throbbing of vivacious injury followed, originating from the exposed layers of damaged skin-

Sweat stung her eyes. Habit made her blink. Her right eye complied; the left...

Horror followed. Fiery white at the edge almost straight to the centre where molten orange clung deep, just like the length of iron he'd used to blind her for spite and-

Her hold on the State of Veranto wavered like a drunk on route home from a bender at a local tavern. The undeniable understanding of what he'd done worming below her veneer and sending tremors through her weaning link. For a single moment she was too absorbed; for a blink, denial was a fine friend, telling her she could overcome this, that she could still save Iambre and retain her clandestine title to protect her friend from harm - then Mitail was suddenly there again, yanking her face straight, rapidly trapping her with a fist in her hair, so that she did not have time to cry out in protest as he jammed a funnel-shaped wedge between her lips with rough disregard for teeth or gums.

Cursing with difficulty, she protested, straining against his ministrations, fearing she'd soon be bearing more injuries, more burns...

"Oh, you must relax, grey-eyes," Zulavi's voice reached her from beyond the bubble she felt trapped in, "If you don't relax, how can you experience the total pleasure when the God reaches for you?

"Still, as I suspected, and as you promised, the State of Veranto is not in- ductive to this form of trial. You cannot give yourself when you do not let go; when your screams do not form the song of proper worship to reach His ears. This will all be for nothing unless you let up. Would you not just let up?!"

With a soothing noise, Zulavi reached out to cup her chin like a benign Wise-Woman and a shudder of shameful but strange relief went through Solan- cei for the respite. Her elaborate wheeze became a shuddering breath. Then an- other. Then Zulavi ran a finger across the injuries on her cheek, saying, "You are so resilient. Your scars will be magnificent: I will rub the wounds with viper's blood: it brings out colour – but first: we cannot carry on like this. I will relieve you of that pesky bond with the Veranto and then you will feel Anchan'Chi's touch and I will get my answers. Are you ready, grey-eyes?"

"Meer'ron," she whispered, "No..."

Body growing liquid when all her fear melted the former ice to further di- lute the already thin blood in her veins, Solancei's handicapped gaze flashed from Zulavi to the man with the lank ponytail.

Though she was on her back, her world seemed to sway and tilt. Somehow she felt out of sync with her own body. Part of her registered that Zulavi still gripped the tool that had blinded her but it held no 'substance' to her. Mitail's hands made her growl; she heard him cuss, imagined the grip intensify, and she felt an acute stab of danger, then hopeless frustration. *Perhaps if she'd not been stupid enough to let herself get tied to this thing; perhaps if she'd fought the Regu- lators harder; perhaps if Klaas had not wasted her hard-fought strength on anger before realising that Solancei had not been deliberately defying her; perhaps... per- haps...*

Not caring about her hair, Solancei twisted herself in the opposite direction of Mitail so abruptly that his hold on the wedge disappeared and she expelled it from her mouth with a defiant curse.

"You treasonous bastard!" she snarled and spat, not knowing if she meant the words for Mitail or Simaro or Swentor, but it hardly mattered. Simarovien Zulavi laughed softly at her display and all the while the sounds of her own ragged breath, loud in her ears, accompanied the commotion and the clank of

rattling chains as she fought the battle she'd already lost. Her range of movement was naturally stunted, and Mitail – clearly aware of his master's unforgiving mind - retrieved the funnel with a snarl...

The ensuing fight was unfair, of course. It was marred by Solancei's hopeless
frenzy and her rank terror, but strong fingers dug aggressively into her cheeks,
forcing her mouth open. She tasted metallic blood and hot sweat and grey ash
but it was better than the nectar-sweet residue from before. She yelped and
thrashed, twisting her head to and thru, but hard fingers and dirty nails came at
her: repeatedly scratching, pulling, *bruising her new injuries...*

Registering that their actions would have draped her in pain without the
Veranto, part of her knew that she was battling something far more important
than an eye now - *for without the Veranto... without it...*

Eventually, her head was seized in a vice - she did not know by whom – but
they forced it tight against the rack: the offending pair of hands stronger than
she had power to fight. Brash defiance or lies – dignity was long gone - but she
did not care what Zulavi might or mightn't read into that, nor did she care now,
how her reaction could only serve to confirm his knowledge that the Meer'ron
would cripple her. *Every moment was another blink of protection for herself and
Iambre now; a heartbeat for Klaas to-*

She hadn't time to finish the sentiment in her own mind. Curses billowed
all around; their hands were like spiders all over her face and trussed up like
this, she could not thwart them any longer. Inevitably, someone jammed the
funnel-like piece of wood back between her lips - the brute action knocking
her teeth as they half-succeeded, the rasping sensation making her feel like a
wrench as the funnel was gradually forced deeper, her jaw cramping under the
strain.

From then everything a blur, meaning fled: they could've been three, they
could've been six, it held no relevance and thus she did not know either who
started pouring the Meer'ron, but suddenly it was happening: the first few
drops sloshing messily to the side of the funnel, trailing a dark shiny track down
the outer rim before dripping onto her cheek. Then 'whomever' gained better
control and the drink started flowing in earnest then.

She gagged; the unmistakable, musky smell of the hated concentrate
reached her nose just a split heartbeat before a thick stream of the sweet

draught itself entered her mouth. *She refused to swallow. Someone pinched her nose tightly...*

Entering on the end of a desperate gasp for air, the thick, bitter-sweet liquid filtered down her throat regardless of her protest; she was coughing but the hands would not let up; she swallowed... swallowed again... *once, then twice...*

She felt tears spill; did not care. She hated them all; hated what they were doing; hated how she had wound up here; hated how Klaas had not warned her of Zulavi; hated how she'd been too craven to tell Klaas the truth about the 'glitches'; hated how she was losing control; hated her own weakness; *hated how resignation had already set in...*

Then new feelings fluttered and ripped. It didn't seem possible but rather than being the foul drink she'd feared, the fluid Meer'ron felt beyond wonderful in her dry throat – so good in fact that after the initial couple of resentful mouthfuls, her trauma seemed a little more removed than before. *So wonderful in fact, that-*

Somewhere above her, she heard Swentor laugh: a soft chuckle of triumph and the sound cut through her complacency like a dagger edged with Dragon Silver. Remembering what the draught would do to her, she wanted to thrash madly against his hands – but her strength was long gone and instead, she lacked... *everything.*

Sobbing with desperation, suddenly more afraid than she'd ever been in her entire life, Solancei spat out the next hated mouthful only to find herself unable to stop from drinking the following one and she both sobbed and bucked as their strength continued to hold her in place.

The Realm forgive her: she could not persist! Zulavi was going to undo everything she'd worked a lifetime to achieve and afterwards he'd destroy everything she'd ever held dear, and he would not care when the world turned to dust and war!

She sobbed again, then choked as more of the poison cloaked her throat, flowing... flowing... And yet she drank it now: one more noxious gulp after the other; sobbed and spit; was forced to drink again. *Over and over; despair permeating.*

Gods strike her down – but she hoped Anchan'Chi would take her now: take her and then rip out her throat for the lies she'd told in His name! This disaster would be worse than any of her childhood losses and all of the ensuing nightmares - because this would be all her fault! Her fault!

She did not quite know when the flow of liquid finally stopped but she was suddenly just aware that she was no longer drinking.

How much had she drunk? Did it even matter? All at once, Solancei was no longer so sure. Something warm was spreading through her body and it made her feel instantly better as it rolled along her limbs, at first languid and sensuous, but soon releasing a sensation of a rapid fire that ate along the path of her veins, cancelling out every raw nerve, banishing all her remaining feelings of dread and fear.

Too oddly, that part felt a little like floating into the State of Veranto - which was impossible of course, because she was already holding onto that Link like a dying person holding onto the comforting hand of an old friend.

And what an impossible analogy! Solancei wanted to laugh. *Because she was definitely not dying! How could she be, when she was buzzing everywhere?*

The hiss of steam cut through her dreamlike thoughts. Zulavi and Mitail were burning the holy runes of 'infinity' and 'servitude' into the tender skin on her neck and down the insides of her biceps, interspersed with the symbol of the God, over and over, but she still did not feel the pain and the stench barely touched her now; time was in flux. On and off she was floating in darkness. She sensed fluids trail over her hip; on one occasion hot iron tore into her, ripping a screech from her throat as agony flashed then died, but the physical pain of the other burns and cuts never touched her, nor did they sting – or maybe they did but she was long since fuzzy on the order of things. *The edges of her vision had become tinted. A pink-laced red...*

With a curious sort of insight, Solancei realised that up to this moment, she'd been frozen to the core somehow – yet now it was no longer so. A delicious heat tingled everywhere, thawing her, healing her, and then she gradually began to relax.

The world had become a blur. *When? Was she drunk?*

Curiously dizzy, vision oddly slurred, she remembered then of having been told that this was how people felt when they got sloshed. For mercy, it was not as unpleasant as she'd been led to believe. *For mercy...*

She almost giggled to herself. *Gods... Klaas would be livid. Klaas would not allow it. But rats to the sour old woman!*

Barely aware that she was laughing under her breath, Solancei became vaguely conscious of the fact that she was able to move her head freely again.

Why she hadn't been able to do so before was an uncertain memory but it didn't matter. Her lips were buzzing.

For a heartbeat, she recalled how it had felt kissing Lazrin Sandborn but the memory tangled and dissolved; Iambre had told her how *her* lips would be buzzing after kissing Bilan and how she liked the feeling and Solancei had scolded her and-

An acute shot of danger fluttered through her. *Iambre... her friend was in danger, but...*

Solancei lost her train of thought as her eyes seemed to shut all of their own. Interestingly, her mind was vividly coloured in the same pink shades, setting her ablaze with the same warmth and comfort that had just rolled through her veins. It overruled the strange tug of her sixth sense that left her with a fleeting notion that something terrible had happened, but since the exact memory failed to materialise, it was probably of little concern to her anyway.

From a world far away, a voice brought her back and she opened her eyes to see who, but her vision was oddly impaired. A blurry face floated above her, briefly, hidden behind that thick glass wall which separated her from that other place. *She felt like heated marchpane but didn't care.* Equally thick voices spoke unintelligible words just beyond her ability to comprehend, but perhaps she could float beyond to visit them? After all, it made sense to do that, given the small point that she had no body anymore.

With a slow languid grin, Solancei got upright as if to dispute the fact - only to crash down in a heap as though her body was a boneless husk. Strangely, she pondered the curious fact that she hadn't felt herself fall until something hard and substantial hit her full face. *Was that... was that the ground?*

Pitted and rough, the chill surface spread below her outstretched body and still she couldn't seem to care.

Where had she been before? She felt peculiar. Surprise made her gasp. *Had she just fallen down? Yes, that was it, or...*

The out-of-nowhere light distracted.

A beautiful vista, the sudden appearance of a glorious evening sky spread above her: deep reds and oranges smeared across the magenta heavens with just a hint of deeper purple: a truly magnificent display of colour that seemed to bleed into the horizon to become one with the barren lands. *She was on the ground here too.* It distracted, but the skyline was drawing her gaze over and over...

It was barely a contest. She'd always adored sunsets.

The spectacle was too alluring and Solancei fell into the twilight sky, seemingly stretching on and on until only the lengthening shadows and the deeper shades of indigo and greying purple remained to touch the landscape. Contentment filled her, yet slowly – *ever so slowly* - a fey coldness associated with more than nightfall, began to steal forth. *It brought the memory of fear: a memory she did not like; a memory that disturbed...*

She froze. *Something sinister was moving in the periphery of her vision. Something she'd known before, and-*

Limbs weakening with creeping terror, she heard her own breath still just as a shadow whipped forward: unforgiving like a viper tricked from its nest - and even with the light weaning, one look showed her enough. *Hyatt'Raah!*

Solancei recoiled from the monster as though someone had punched her. The creature she'd hoped to never again see: the monster of claws and teeth, all fire-red hide stretched tightly over ascetic muscular limps - leapt towards her – its grotesquely elongated features cast in feral abandon, as the ridged tail whipped just once like that of an angered cat.

Crying out in wordless fear, Solancei found her wits, retreated with a scramble and rolled to evade as the thing pounced for her, but another beast set upon her from that very direction and she flailed, falling back towards the first monster.

Slicing claws raked at her. It missed by a hairsbreadth...

Crashing down, she screeched in pain as her body set on fire from multiple injuries. It stole her last air. The trail of claw marks across her chest was like deep runnels of fire inked into her skin. *Mercy, she though the Hyatt had missed her, but now she hurt! The two creatures stalked nearer, death and hunger in their flat soulless eyes.*

She tried to get up but she couldn't breathe!

The creatures were close enough for her to distinguish the revolting carrion stench that seemed to pollute the air around them. They were watching her: perhaps hoping she'd run for sport but when she didn't move quick enough, sickles attached to long-fingered, claw-like paws, raked towards her like projectiles as they half-stalked, half-hopped to circle ever closer.

Solancei pushed to get herself up off the ground one final time but from the way those narrow pinstripe pupils seemed to contract even further as the Hyatt'Raah tracked her gaze, she knew herself already dead. *It was maybe deserved, a part of her whispered with fey satisfaction. She'd failed; she'd become an oathbreaker too and traitors burned. She should die!*

As she looked away, the Hyatt struck. The precision of jaw and teeth merciless as they tore her skin and ripped into flesh

The world became red. *A drowning ruby red of blood and beauty...*

WAKING UP, SHIVERING in a pool of icy sweat and rank fear, reality seemed just another illusion to Solancei yet the formations of agony slicing through her broken body were too complete not to exist in true life.

A tremor followed, visceral, stirring old pain and new. Something was gnawing in the pit of her belly: a strange kind of hunger almost.

She took it to herald that the Meer'ron poison was wearing off and it seemed she was correct. Soon the empty feeling spread tendrils into her veins, her muscles, and sinew, whilst in her core, a knot of unknown urges had already begun stirring.

In the back of her throat she tasted piercing herbs disguised as vanilla and honey, and like the decay of a rotten corpse left too long, the idea revolted her.

She gagged, then regretted it. They'd filled her with enough Meer'ron to floor a horse; mercifully she'd taken no time passing out and recalled most of the ritual hurt they'd subjected her to, only as vague passages in between dreams of longing and harrowing nightmares. *The poison had both sheltered and destroyed, yet-*

Another tremor rattled through her, needles following, but she forced herself to lie still. *She recalled she'd taken a long time to die - those blood-red Hyatts ripping into their feast with a kind of ecstasy she could only now put a name to because they were gone and their bite clearly never anything but a drug-induced hallucination – or a 'ride through the Red Haze' as Zulavi had called it. However, if she had not truly died, the lingering pain could be synonymous with only one thing...*

No longer chained or restrained she rolled over, the effort laborious, her rewards none, as the pain of multiple ritual cuts and burned cyphers of scripture and madness flashed and screamed with terrible permanence across the once-unmarked skin of the entire left side of her body.

The understanding was too vivid to compete with the broken ribs and she moaned under her breath, the grey light diffuse, but yet a terrible reminder of daylight and thereby just enough for her to see, but...

But she refused to focus, because to focus-

With a half-sob, half-gasp she cascaded back into black despair, the knowledge that Zulavi had scarred her beyond the need to buy another mirror still blanching when habit made her search for her Art to reach for a Link, only to find a cold void where once the symbolic gate she'd taken years to fashion should've marked its presence.

It made her quiver again, but the truth remained; the truth, that somewhere in the depths of her impossible nightmarish hallucinations, the State of Veranto has slipped from her grasp as unobtrusively as the fine grains of sand emptying into the bottom half of an hourglass!

It left her nothing. Nothing but a hard floor and a memory of loss that seemed just as mentally scarring as the physical damage done by Zulavi.

NOW... *later*... much, much later, someone came to her.

Asking questions again: bewildering, longwinded questions. She failed to care, though eventually soured with the need of what her body demanded, she inevitably surrendered replies - though by that stage her mind was too afloat and her recall strangely uncertain.

And somehow the answers she offered only angered; the men's words and actions became repeatedly rife with threats, but their purpose remained hazy too: distant; unhooked from her world. Nothing seemed real. Nothing that was, except for the gnawing unnatural hunger in her belly, which made it doubly hard to focus – and besides, *to focus*...

More than once, she was mercifully thrown back into oblivion, her injuries so easily pulling her over the edge that she'd lose herself, but the men would return regardless. *Taunting her, punishing, tempting...* they'd play odd games, often as not withholding the next draught of Meer'ron till she floundered so badly in withdrawal that they appeared to have no choice but to reluctantly administer a doze.

Yet the questions never ceased. Her craving the poison amused them - she understood this, but she was confused. Always confused – and hence maybe not coherent.

She angered them again. *And again. And...*

But maybe... maybe she did not anger them all the time, she sensed. And maybe she was a coward but she wanted to escape into that red universe brought to her in the form of this sticky drink they controlled, for here the Demonai would kill her. *Again. And again.* And the deep inner part of her that screamed against this downward spiral she'd been set upon, was perhaps only too happy to embrace the illusion of the Red Haze as though it were real, because mercy... if she prayed hard enough, and long enough, then perhaps... then perhaps maybe the next time would be the time she did not awaken from the nightmares, because soon...

...soon she would make herself an oath breaker; she was losing this hour by hour, draught by draught, question by question...

Too exhausted to resist, the thought fluttered through her mind that she hoped they'd burn her and Zulavi at the same stake: his screams would certainly entertain-

More Meer'ron trickled into her mouth, raising the notion of bliss, but it was stolen by frustration and slighted sense of fulfilment as the flow halted and stopped. *This was not enough to tip her over the edge and so the would-be ecstasy of death would most certainly elude her!*

Tendrils of pain stole through her limbs. *Injury or withdrawal?* She couldn't tell today. Then somebody was kissing her on the lips, invading her mouth with their breath and tongue to steal an illicit taste of poison, quickly catching her chin with sword-calloused fingers to still weak objections when she pushed sluggishly to be left alone, then proclaiming her a 'good girl'; blaspheming; telling her between subtle sounds of enjoyment that if Anchan'Chi did not see fit to claim His Bride, others soon would.

More Meer'ron followed finally. *Was it a new hour? A new day?*

She managed to swallow the offered trickle this time: as per usual it was not enough to satisfy the gnawing, not enough to still the subsequent tremor as it travelled down her limbs, yet something felt different; her inner voice noticed just a spear's width of change in the time before the haze seemed to lift, then...

Pain shimmered through her, a forerunner of much worse, though for once parting the fogs in her mind to bring a sense of unwanted lucidity. A terrible sense of doom seemed to roll over her. She couldn't be sure, but...

But had she just spoken Iambre's name?

Weary, she looked into a stranger's face. His gaze was intense. Demanding. Questioning. Yet at the same time, something she'd said had brought to life an expression of halting triumph, for his non-descript features seemed to twitch on the cusp true pleasure as he appeared to be searching her for something unvoiced, but specific. *His intensity reminded her of Zulavi, but his nose was wider than Simaro's; more bulbous...*

A moment longer everything seemed to swim in the balance. She watched his eyes grow strangely hooded as though he was visually searching her for foul play. A moment passed, then his Zanzier-pallid face altered, a savage smile suddenly locking into a place of certainty.

"Got ya, blade-witch." the smiling stranger exclaimed, pale eyes oddly fervour-bright as he leaned in to target her lips with a hard triumphant kiss that momentarily ruined the smile before he pulled clear.

"Gods rot, how you've been drowning," he whispered, the smile flickering back to life.

Eager gaze rapidly perusing her as if he needed to make certain of something unvoiced, his attention slipped sporadically over her wealth of injuries and she imagined a brief flare of regret in the slant of his eyes...

Then he appeared to shake himself. On the edge of his words a slithering tone of amazement caught hold, as he continued ,"Gods be great - we thought perhaps Anchan'Chi might have claimed you for His after all; we thought... guts and tits, we thought your sanity spent but seems we finally got ya, Bride; it seems we finally broke you - so now... now you will talk sense. And now... well, now Zulavi will finally pay out that bonus and he might even allow Mitail to carve his own initials into your feet, but that's between the two of you!"

Straightening slowly, the man hooked a stray lock of mousy-blond hair behind one ear and Solancei was assaulted by a stab of icy needles. *The pain was bearable, but the fear this time no longer imagined, it seemed.*

Visage turning artfully pensive, the man used a thumb to gently mop away a forgotten trail of Meer'ron from her chin, in the process jarring the raised welts on her cheek to make her hiss.

He ignored the weakness.

Considering the glistening dew on the summit of his digit, then offering Solancei another brief look of assessment, he sucked the unsavoury mix of fluids from his finger with a subtle shiver of pleasure.

Opening his eyes after a moment, the timbre of casual enquiry in his voice almost matching that of polite conversation, he said, "So by the way... I know of only one Princess and by coincidence, her name also happens to be Iambre del'Dulac Isthalani Actarione. Tell me correct, Bride: how exactly is it that you've come to now the very Heiress of Ostravah herself? And also, how exactly is it that you think you will escape this Nisela'Cha's armpit of a black dung hole to kill us all?"

Thank you for reading!
The story will continue in Episode 7: The Lure of an Ancient Fable
Available now!

Post Script from the author

H i there!
   If you enjoyed this book I'd really love it if you could take just two minutes to leave a review on your media of choice(s).

   It's matters because not only do I get feedback on my product, which is invaluable for me to learn and grow as an author, but it may also help other readers understand if this book is for them and – very importantly – that it's okay to take a chance on an indie publication.

AND DON'T FORGET...

   For extra insider info, updates, freebies, exclusive offers and giveaways, you can also allow me to keep in contact by signing up to my newsletter by typing in the link below, or visiting my official author web site.

   https://mailchi.mp/486a3a8674b0/themissingshield
   https://www.llthomsen.com

Feeling curious about the world of Ostravah?

For glossaries, maps, and more, please visit my official author website on
www.llthomsen.com[1]

Also feel free to contact me on
llthomsen@themissingshield.com

Or visit me on -
www.twitter.com/LLThomsen1[2]
www.facebook.com/linda.thomsen.12979[3]
www.facebook.com/themissingshield/[4]
www.facebook.com/themissingshield/[5]
www.instagram.com/llthomsen/?hl=en[6]

---

1. http://www.llthomsen.com

2. http://www.twitter.com/LLThomsen1

3. http://www.facebook.com/linda.thomsen.12979

4. http://www.facebook.com/themissingshield/

5. http://www.facebook.com/themissingshield/

6. http://www.instagram.com/llthomsen/?hl=en

The Missing Shield Series
This story begins in Episode 1 of The Missing Shield.
Below is the full list of books in the series in order of release.

> A Change of Rules – Episode 1
> Unexpected Bargain – Episode 2
> A Perspective of Death – Episode 3
> Running the Gauntlet – Episode 4
> Notions of Risk – Episode 5
> The Final Card - Episode 6
> The Lure of an Ancient Fable – Episode 7

And coming up soon...
> All in a Day's Work – Episode 8
> The Way Star –Episode 9
> All Thieves' Honour – Episode 10
> The Neidar Ba'raie – Episode 11
This will complete The Missing Shield – Vol 1 of The Veil Keepers Quest.

www.ingramcontent.com/pod-product-compliance
Lightning Source LLC
Chambersburg PA
CBHW020136180626
46810CB00004B/1589